NEW YORK TIMES AND USA TODAY BESTSELLING AUTHOR

LORA LEIGH

SOUL DEEP

ELLORA'S CAVE®
ROMANTICA® PUBLISHING

What the critics are saying...

ഇ

"SOUL DEEP is steamy, sexy, heartrending and completely riveting." ~ *Love Romances*

"If you've become hooked on the Breeds series, you won't be disappointed by this book." ~ *Road to Romance*

"Readers who love the Feline Breed Series will like this book. You revisit many old friends from the previous books and one gets an update on their current lives as a bonus."
~ *Mon-Boudoir*

"*Soul Deep*, is one story you won't be able to put down and it just proves to me again and again why Lora Leigh is quickly becoming one of my favorite paranormal writers."
~ *Fallen Angel Reviews*

An Ellora's Cave Romantica Publication

www.ellorascave.com

Soul Deep

ISBN 9781419954627
ALL RIGHTS RESERVED.
Soul Deep Copyright © 2004 Lora Leigh
Edited by Sue-Ellen Gower.
Cover art by Syneca.

This book printed in the U.S.A. by Jasmine–Jade Enterprises, LLC.

Trade paperback Publication September 2007

SOUL DEEP

ഔ

Dedication

∞

To the readers!
For all your emails, your encouragement and support
This one is for all of you!

Trademarks Acknowledgement

∞

The author acknowledges the trademarked status and trademark owners of the following wordmarks mentioned in this work of fiction:

Glock: Glock Inc. Corporation

Grand Cherokee: Daimler Chrysler Corporation

Jacuzzi: Jacuzzi Inc. Corporation

Lexus: Toyota Jidosha Kabushiki Kaisha Corporation Japan 1

Teflon: E. I. Du Pont De Nemours and Company

Chapter One

๙

Word received from the Feline Breed compound reports that Major Dash Sinclair of the United States Army has tested positive as a Wolf Breed. Major Sinclair is the first known Wolf Breed to survive the extermination when word first broke of their creation a year ago.

American Military and Science communities are quick to assure the press and government alike that there could be very few of these missing Breeds, and that the odds of such escape were so astronomical at the time, that if there were others, it would indeed be a miracle.

Labs around the world that were creating and raising the Wolf Breed soldiers, eradicated their creations on executive order of the head of the Genetics Council, none other than former Vice President, Douglas Finnell. Investigations into the Council members through computers and records seized during a coordinated strike against discovered labs revealed a cruelty and complete lack of human morality in the creation and training of these unique individuals. The atrocities performed by the Genetics Council, their guards and scientists has been labeled by many as one of the most horrific crimes committed against living beings.

Operation Indifference was a major strike that crossed international boundaries and borders, and threw light on the depth of moral depravity that created, trained and murdered men women and children who were being trained as killers and advanced soldiers to use against the general population in coming years. A private army that would know no mercy.

But as scientists around the world are now claiming, the Breeds rescued from the concentration camp-like conditions are showing an instinctive, pre-selective inner honor, or law of nature. Records and training logs clearly prove that the Genetics Council was failing in their directive. They created the perfect soldier, but one who refused

9

to kill innocents, and one who would, in the face of great pain, uphold the personal honor that had somehow been established. In all Breeds but one. The Coyote Breeds. Jailors, in some cases trainers and executors, the Coyote was the Council's eventual triumph, some sources report.

Unfortunately, as Operation Indifference commenced and these heavily fortified labs were attacked, their creations were slaughtered; men, women and children murdered to prevent the freedom of these unique, genetically altered humans.

Major Sinclair's story of escape from the compound at a mere ten years of age, and his subsequent journey through social services as an orphan and ward of the state has raised many questions about the survival of other hidden Breeds, though. Breeds who escaped the initial destruction through sheer determination and luck.

The Genetics Council was dismantled with the help of Merinus Tyler, wife and proclaimed mate to Callan Lyons, leader of the Feline Breeds who escaped from a New Mexico compound more than a decade ago. Since revealing themselves to the world, the Feline Breeds have worked exclusively, around the world, towards finding those of their brethren still being held captive in the labs that created them. Smaller, secretive labs that still work to perfect the genetic selection that will create the bloodthirsty, logical, cold-blooded killers the Council sought.

To date, more than a hundred Feline Breeds now occupy the former Council compound in Virginia and are making inroads in creating a comfortable atmosphere for the former captives who make their way there.

The Pure Blood societies are on the rise now, though. What we once called white supremacists are now becoming blood supremacists and demanding the incarceration of the Breeds to keep the genetic alterations the Breeds carry, out of the general population. Newly elected President, Vernon Marion, has scoffed at such demands, proclaiming the Breeds to be no more a risk than Native American, Irish or other foreign nationalities were centuries before. But the fight isn't over.

As reported, attacks on Breeds and the Breed compound have been escalating over the months and this new development, a Breed *living among us, unknown, as familiar to the men he fought with as the guy next door, has raised complications President Marion will have face. Adopted children and known orphans have arrived in vast numbers to doctors' offices around the world, demanding genetic testing to prove they aren't carrying the Breed DNA. Supremacists groups are now demanding this test become required in all doctors' offices, hospitals, and health facilities.*

It also raises the question that if Wolf and Feline escapees are now roaming the world, what of the Coyotes that were bred to be their jailors? Reports state the Coyote Breeds were bred, raised and trained to enhance the DNA that many Native American scholars have indicated could exclude them from what is being called Breed Honor, the instinctive code of nature all Breeds so far claim. If the Coyote, in its natural state, truly has no soul, then will the man created from that DNA, have a conscience?

With Breed Law now in the Senate, scheduled for vote within weeks, the questions being raised are becoming more than just the Right to Life. Breed Law, in effect, will give Breeds autonomy.

It will allow for the creation of a Breed offensive titled Strike and Defend where specially selected groups will, in effect, have full government approval to kill, without prejudice, any group or groups that strike against the Breed Compound or selected Breed reserves. One of the laws presently on the table also allows for the execution of any government employed or private citizen found to have knowingly and/or willingly played a part in the death or attack of such Breed facilities as well.

It also includes a law that many Senators are currently debating even more heavily than the Strike and Defend statute. A law simply titled, Right to Mate. This law, Senators are stating, is much too vague for clear understanding. As stated in the statute, a Breed Mate, defined as any male or female considered mated by the Breed Ruling Table, will, in effect, be under Breed Law, and under the jurisdiction of any and all Breed sanctions that may be imposed.

This law, if voted in, will give a Breed society complete jurisdiction over itself, with no governmental influence for the period of fifty years. The Breed Ruling Table will be comprised of several Breed leaders, including Callan Lyons, who will head the lawmaking

11

body, Kane Tyler, brother to Merinus Tyler and the driving force behind the strike against the labs, and Senator Sam Tyler, a proponent of Breed Law, as well as several scientists who have already become permanent additions to the Breed compound in Virginia since the birth of Callan and Merinus's son, David Lyons, last year.

Proponents of the Law are assuring the public and the press alike that all countermeasures are in place with the Law to ensure that both the genetically altered Breeds and the normal population can live in harmony. They state they are aware of the fears of the general population and are striving to alleviate them.

But, have we, mankind, evolved yet to a point where such differences can be accepted and lived with? Can a Breed move amongst us, free of the prejudice that we've shown to other races in the past? Scholars and historians alike are questioning the possibility...

Chapter Two

∞

Halloween. Trick or Treat. Parties, ghosts and goblins. Amanda loved it.

She laughed as she stood at the door and gave out the treats to the pint-sized little masqueraders, remarked on costumes and complimented cherub-cheeked little monsters on the creations their parents had come up with for them.

The air was crisp and fresh, the fall evening invigorating and cheery. There was nothing about Halloween that she didn't love. It was the one event that she wasn't required to show up at her father's home and play nice as she conversed with boring politicians and aged lotharios. She could relax at home, watch a movie and see the joy in the eyes of the children who visited her front stoop for the treats she had to give out.

Dressed in the long, red demoness outfit, she drew her fair amount of interested glances from the men, but was still well covered enough to allow for the mothers to socialize with her comfortably. The red, long dress was thin, but not transparent, flowing from her waist to her hips in a cloud of red perfection. The snug bodice laced beneath her breasts, while the voile material cupped and hugged her breasts. Her long, brown hair was left loose and falling to her waist, and small red horns sat atop her head.

It was her standard Halloween treat-giving costume. She felt sexy, alive, independent. Especially this year. Her first official year away from the strictures of her family. At least, almost away from it.

"Hi, Ms. Marion." Kylie Brock bounced up the steps, her little devil costume displayed as the little girl gave her a gap-toothed smile. "I look just like you."

Amanda glanced at her mother. Tammy Brock was a slender, up-and-coming young lawyer who lived several houses down. With laughing blue eyes and a wry sense of humor, the older woman rolled her eyes at her daughter.

"Well you sure do, Kylie." Amanda bent her knees, bringing herself down to the level of the child as she placed a handful of treats in the little girl's opened bag. "Have you been scaring everyone out of candy tonight?"

The little girl glanced at the top of Amanda's head. She sighed deeply.

"Oh yes. I have lots of candy. But Mommy couldn't find me horns like yours."

The children had loved her outfit when she wore it to school the day before for the Halloween party. The horns especially.

"She couldn't?" Amanda reach up to straighten the specially made horns she had found in a unique little gift store while shopping with her sister in New York.

"I looked everywhere," Tammy Brock laughed. "Even the costume supply stores. They must think I'm a madwoman."

Amanda chuckled with her.

"Tell you what, I bought several pairs." She lifted the horns from her head and secured the small combs that anchored them in place in the red wig Kylie wore.

Her eyes rounded as her pale face flushed in pleasure.

"They're mine?" she asked in amazement, her gray eyes shining with happiness. "Just mine?"

"Just yours." Amanda smiled, accepting the little girl's excited hug as the mother stared back at her thankfully.

"Thank you, Amanda" she whispered as Kylie bounced down the steps to show off her treasure to her friends. "You just made her night."

"How has she been doing?" Kylie had been diagnosed with a rare blood disorder the year before, and it had been a hard journey for her and her parents.

"Good days, bad days," Tammy sighed. "I almost didn't bring her out tonight, but she was so looking forward to it."

Amanda nodded. "Let me know if you need anything." She hugged the other woman tightly, her heart breaking at the pressure she knew her new friend must be under.

"I will," Tammy nodded. "And you take care too. I imagine being the President's daughter right now is coming with more downs than ups?"

Amanda drew back, her lips twisting with the irony of the other woman's comment.

"It has its days," she admitted with a laugh, plying more candy into open bags as several more children approached her.

After the mess of the Presidential election, the protests of Breed Law, Breed Rights, and Breed everything else, she was due a break. Her own job had become a joke in the past year. Where she had once been a well-respected member of the community, she was now a sounding board for political rhetoric from the school principal down to her sixth grade students and their parents.

If that wasn't bad enough, the Secret Service agents who accompanied her to work and back were really starting to bug her. She wasn't the damned President, and she was getting just slightly frustrated with the problems it was beginning to cause her. They acted like rabid guard dogs.

"Amanda, could I use your little girls' room?" Tammy suddenly asked quietly, a tense smile twisting her lips. "I'm about to die and I don't want have to take Kylie home. I'll just be a moment."

"Sure." Amanda glanced back in the house. "Down the hall on the left."

"I'll be right back." She moved quickly past her and headed into the house. "Kylie should be just fine with her friends for a second if you'll watch her."

Amanda glanced at the little girl. "Go. I'll watch her," she laughed. Kylie was still showing off the horns.

Amanda leaned against the doorframe, watching her closely. She loved children, and one day imagined she would have one of her own. At times she wondered why she waited. She could have married twenty times over, if she was willing to settle for one of the men offering. Plain, boring little momma's boys, she thought with a sigh, knowing it would never work.

"Thanks." Tammy moved past her moments later, her eyes darting nervously to the sidewalk where Kylie chatted with her friends.

"Take it easy, Tammy." Amanda frowned at the nervous smile the mother cast her before she moved quickly down the steps and urged her little girl further along the street.

The house beside Amanda's was dark, no lights to welcome the little trick-or-treaters. She frowned at the door to the other half of her duplex and sniffed in distain.

The Secret Service unit her father had assigned her was camped there. Blockheads.

She closed the door after handing out the last of her treats and turned back to the living room of her spacious duplex. She came to an abrupt stop. Her eyes widened in shock at the black-clad forms standing in her hallway.

Her gaze swung to the alarm system on the other wall, too far away for her to trigger the manual alert, but she could see the red light that indicated the back door had been deactivated. Dear God. Tammy had to have deactivated the alarm. But why?

Okay, so where were the blockheads then? she thought frantically. They should have received an alert that the back door was unlocked as well as the front while she was outside.

They were so anal she would have thought they would check it out immediately.

"Can I help you?" she squeaked, hysterically amused at the polite phrase that escaped her lips as she backed toward the door she had just closed. In one blinding second she realized she was pretty screwed.

There were four of them. That was more than her self-defense training was going to handle at once, that was for sure. Masks covered their faces but nothing could hide the feral hatred in their eyes. Amanda swallowed tightly, wondering at her chances of escape. It didn't look good.

"Yes, you can." One of them stepped forward, pale blue eyes glittering ferally as he lifted the gun he held loosely in his hand and pointed it at her head. "You can come quietly, or I can shoot you. Your choice."

"I get a choice." She blinked with mocking innocence. "Oh, wow. Can I think about it a while?"

She almost winced at the sarcasm. Bad move. Sarcasm and guns did not mix.

Cold blue eyes narrowed on her as he cocked the gun, the sound ricocheting through her body and causing her to flinch in dread.

"Do you really want to take that risk, Ms. Marion?" he asked her softly. "It could be deadly."

She drew in a deep breath, swallowing tightly. She hated choices. A bullet or perhaps a fate worse than death? If she was very, very lucky a gunshot would only hurt like hell and draw enough attention... Nope, silencer. Damn.

She stood silent, still, facing them as she caught sight of the light from the corner of her eye. She wasn't going to just let them calmly take her. Only God knew who they were.

He took another step and she jumped. Her hand slapped down on the switch as she jumped for the door, pushing back the lock as she twisted the doorknob and screamed for all she was worth. A second after the sound escaped her throat, darkness descended.

Damn. Dying wasn't going to be fun...

Chapter Three

ဢ

Babysitting duty sucked. Kiowa sat back in the seat of the luxurious Lexus and watched the little demoness hand out candy like royal favors and stifled a growl of arousal. He had been at this for a week now, and her effect on him was damned inconvenient. And that costume wasn't helping matters any.

She smiled at the kids, her face lighting up with pleasure at each one that came to her door, only to become smoothly polite while talking to the parents. She held herself aloof, in control, but he could sense a fire simmering inside her.

Damned woman, watching her hadn't been his brightest move. He should have told Dash Sinclair to take a damned hike when he tracked him down and asked him to join this insanity. The world was not going to accept Breeds. President Marion could vote a hundred Breed Laws in and it wasn't going to make a difference. They were too different. But Dash and Callan Lyons were certain it could happen. Just as they were certain Kiowa could help.

He snorted at that. A coyote consorting with lions and wolves. What was next?

He shifted in the leather seat, readjusting his cock and grimacing at the engorged length. Just what he needed, a hard-on for the President's sweet little daughter. That was guaranteed to get him hunted and killed like the mangy animal he was created to be, he thought mockingly.

As Kiowa watched the front door, it suddenly swung open, a woman's strangled scream barely reaching him as it closed just as fast. His eyes moved to the door beside her, the duplex her Secret Service unit was using was dark and quiet. No lights came on; no alarm was sounded.

His gaze narrowed as he scanned the nearly deserted street now. Trick-or-treaters were on the street above and below, but there was no one close enough to hear that abrupt cry. Cursing, he pulled the Glock from the waistband of his pants and exited his vehicle quickly. Ducking, he made his way around the cars, then the side of the fence that enclosed the little two-story duplex.

They wouldn't take her out the front door; they would have a car at the back. Dammit, where the hell were her bodyguards, the inept Secret Service detail assigned to her? He personally didn't need this shit. He was supposed to be backup, nothing more, not the damned cavalry.

As he moved through the shadows, rounding the fence carefully, he caught sight of the van and the driver waiting impatiently, a black mask pulled over his face. Kiowa moved through the shadows, inhaling the crisp night air to be certain there were no other guards outside. His vision picked up the driver, but no other signs of a partner in the van.

Stupid. Stupid, he raged silently as he quickly silenced his weapon and fired. The guard slumped over instantly at the same moment the back gate opened. Moving swiftly along the side of the fence, Kiowa jerked the first man past the gate, his arms going around his head and twisting quickly. He dropped the body before the sound of the hollow break finished. The second man, surprised, was just as easy to take out. Ducking, he barely avoided a bullet before firing back and taking out the third. Didn't take those boys long to figure out they were caught, he thought mockingly.

Dogs were howling now, voices raising as the fourth man moved to lay his gun at the temple of the unconscious woman he was holding.

Training could be a wonderful thing, Kiowa thought distantly as extended his arm and fired first, before catching the burden the assailant carried as he fell.

Now what? Goddammit, he didn't need this.

Throwing her over his shoulder, he moved to the van, jerked the dead driver from his seat to the ground and moved in himself. He tossed the girl on the floor of the van, revved the engine and pulled out as lights began to flood the street.

Fuck, he really didn't need this. He was just supposed to watch her. Just watch her and make sure the Goof Troop didn't bungle their job and let the blood supremacists stalking President Marion make an attempt on her.

The Secret Service detail was experienced. They were old hands at protecting First Daughters. The best of the best and they were fucking dead as hell or sleeping on the job and now he was stuck with the Baby Girl.

He'd drop her off somewhere, make a quick little phone call to the nearest police station and that would be that. Easy. Simple.

Bullshit.

If the bastards had got to her this easy then there was some major shit getting ready to hit the fan. No one, but no one, got to the President's daughter that easy without inside help. Shit.

Chapter Four

🔊

An hour later Kiowa pulled the plain white van into the back of a motel he had been circling longer than he cared to admit and lugged his still unconscious burden into the motel room. He hadn't been followed, but he wasn't stupid enough to assume that someone out there wasn't going to be looking for that van fast. An operation that well put together wasn't without its backup.

With quick movements he tied her up and gagged her, though to be honest she didn't look like she was going anywhere soon, but he preferred to err on the side of caution.

She was breathing normally, the bump on her head wasn't overly large, and he had to get rid of that damned van and make a phone call. Dammit, this was the last time frigging time he did Dash or Simon a favor. He knew getting messed up with that quack and his harem was a dumb idea. Really dumb.

He stared down at Sleeping Beauty with a grimace on his face, his hands propped on his hips, and assumed she would live for the brief time he had to be away. He hated taking the chance, but damn if he had a choice. That van was like a beacon to the bad guys, and if blood was going to be shed, he wanted to make damned sure it wasn't his own, he thought as he turned and left the room.

He dumped the van in a junkyard about ten miles out of town before walking to the nearest pay phone and calling a cab. The cabbie picked up a slightly drunk, if not a little belligerent partygoer outside one of the rowdier apartment buildings a few blocks up and drove him to his motel.

There, Kiowa stumbled to his room, opened the door and closed it firmly.

Well, Baby Girl was still breathing at least. And not too hard to look at, but he'd be damned if he wanted the problem.

Pulling his cell phone from his pocket he made the all-important call.

"Hi baby, what can I do for you?" The voice was enough to make any man's dick twitch. Unfortunately, he was a little too pissed to let that organ have any say.

"Get me off," he snapped out the code for an emergency meeting. "I'm at the Lazy Oak Inn. How soon can you be here?"

There was a short silence.

"An hour," she replied, her husky voice showing none of the concern that the situation now warranted. "You have the condom?"

He wanted to roll his eyes at the question. Marion's daughter was considered the shield between success or failure with the most important Breed Law up for vote. That of giving the autonomy, the right to defend and to kill their attackers with no prejudice. If Amanda Marion stayed safe and happy, President Marion would vote with his conscience. But if she was used against him, held as insurance against a nay vote, then the Breeds might as well stick their heads between their legs and kiss their asses goodbye. Marion would sell them up the river for his daughter's life and never give it a second thought.

"I have the fucking condom, dammit," he snarled, glancing at the girl again. "Now get your ass over here."

"You're so romantic," the female voice sighed petulantly. "I might have to spank you for that."

"Be sure to bring the whip then," he grunted. "You're going to need it. Now get moving."

He disconnected the call then sat back in the chair and contemplated his little captive. He snorted at the thought. He would just as soon be sitting outside that little place of hers watching the house for problems than stuck with her now. Simon Quatres and his little fillies better get their asses in gear and get here fast because he wasn't in the mood for this.

Simon could take the President's daughter off his hands in an hour, stash her some place nice and safe and Kiowa would go hunting. He stilled at that thought. What the hell did he even care?

Then his eyes went back to the girl. A smear of blood on her forehead where she had been hit had fury rising inside him all over again. Dammit, there was no need to hit her, he thought. The bastards trying to take her hadn't given a damn if they killed her or not. All they cared about were their fanatical plans and insane prejudices. Yeah, going hunting was a damned good idea. The blood supremacists infecting society now were beginning to wear on his nerves anyway.

He shifted in his chair, grimacing at the hard-on rising in his jeans. The more he looked at her, the harder he was getting. That was a bad thing. Very bad. He had never had a problem separating lust from business, and only when completely necessary did the two overlap. It was damned hard to separate the two while he watched her though. And this was one of those situations when it wasn't just unnecessary but damned stupid.

Sighing wearily, he rose to his feet and removed the gag. She looked to be breathing fine, but he didn't want to take any chances. He slid the cloth free before returning to his chair and once again staring at her. He could get used to looking at her in his bed, he thought.

She did look pretty. Long, long brown hair lay like thick ribbons around her slender body, and that costume was hot as hell. Seductive red, nearly sheer, the bodice snug beneath her breasts, causing them to spill above the low neckline. Soft, silky-looking pale flesh. A rosebud mouth. His dick twitched hard at the sight of that mouth. It was rosy red and tempting as hell. A mouth like that could give a man more ecstasy than he had any right to. Let alone a Breed.

As he watched her, a low moan passed over the tempting curves of her lips, and long lashes fluttered open weakly. He moved from the chair, watching her closely as he eased down on the bed beside her and capped his hand over her mouth just in time.

The muffled scream was accompanied by a frantic bucking of her body as he moved over her, laying against her heavily, staring into eyes such a deep, mysterious hazel that it could make a grown man weep.

Shades of brown, greens and blues collided in those eyes, tiny pinpoints of color that, up close, were almost mesmerizing. They were wide with fear and outrage now. Uh-oh. That hard-on killing him was pressed against her lower belly and, he was certain, was the cause of that outrage and sparks of red-hot fury lighting her eyes.

"Settle down," he muttered, watching her closely, allowing himself to enjoy the feel of the slender body beneath him. "I'm not going to hurt you."

Yeah, she was going to believe that one, he thought, especially with his erection prodding her and those ropes holding her down.

Her muffled scream of outrage against his palm assured him he was right.

"Look lady, if I wanted you dead, you would be dead," he griped. "If I wanted you scared and under control, you'd be gagged as well as tied down. Now I didn't play fucking Sir Galahad so you can bring the roof down and let your attackers' buddies in on the fact that you're alive and well at this point in time. Now do you want to shut the hell up, promise not to scream, or do you want one of my socks shoved in your mouth? Trust me, that's not a good alternative."

She blinked back at him in surprise.

"Are you going to be a good girl now?" he murmured. "Or do I get to lie here until I get tired and use that sock instead?"

Pretty, pretty eyes.

She drew in a deep breath, her nostrils flaring as she stilled beneath him.

"You're gonna be quiet?"

She nodded emphatically.

Watching her suspiciously, he began to lift his hand. Slowly, he moved it back, preparing to lift himself off her if she kept her word. She was soft and sweet to lie on, but he had a feeling... Shit.

Her mouth opened, a piercing scream nearly escaping before he lowered his head and caught it with his lips.

Dumb, dumb idea. Sweet Heaven, her lips were soft, tender, her mouth a warm, seductive cavern beckoning him.

His hands gripped her wrists as slender fingers formed claws. The ropes held her fast, but he gave her his hands to claw, to prick with those delicate little nails. Something to ease the need for violence he knew must be raging inside her.

God, her lips were soft.

He stared into her eyes, feeling the shock clear to the soles of his feet as his tongue licked at the rosebud perfection, tasting something delicate, addictive, feeling a heated madness building in his brain as hunger swelled inside him.

She looked dazed, staring back at him, the blue in her hazel eyes darkening as he licked at her lips again. He only wanted to keep her from screaming, to silence her as fast as possible without hurting her. But he didn't expect this.

He moved his hands, forcing them from her grip so he could burrow into her hair where he could feel it silkiness, hold her in place and delve deeper into her mouth at the same time.

His thumbs pressed against her jaw, controlling her sharp little teeth in case she had a mind to bite, forcing them open enough to thrust his tongue sharply inside her mouth.

God, he ached. His tongue throbbed at the taste of her, prodding at hers as he watched her lashes drift lower, watched her eyes darken.

Sweet, sweet honey filled his senses, tempted his taste buds. Damn she tasted good. Like summer. Innocence. Something he had never known or thought of until he was too old to fool himself into believing it could exist. But it did exist, right here, right now, and the taste of it filled his senses.

Damn, he didn't need this. Before he could weaken further, he jerked his lips back from hers, snagged the gag he had used earlier, a thickly knotted length of torn pillow case and pushed the knot past her parted lips before tying it quickly behind her head, while her muffled screams and frantic struggles pricked at the conscience he wasn't supposed to have.

"Sorry 'bout that." He breathed out roughly, sitting beside her as she stared back at him furiously. "But I really didn't risk my ass so you could scream bloody assed murder and get us both killed."

She was screaming it now as she jerked and bucked against her restraints, her beautiful eyes promising a wealth of retribution as she finally subsided in exhaustion.

"See, I was even going to give you something for that nasty headache I bet you have." He smiled back at her deadly glare. "It hurts pretty bad, huh?"

She looked away, her nostrils flaring with rage, her face flushed as her breasts trembled with agitation. And those were some damned pretty breasts. With perfect tight little nipples

They swelled over the snug red bodice and silky fabric beneath. Firm, plump little globes with surprising hard, spiked nipples. His eyes narrowed on the obvious signs of arousal, his dick flexing beneath his jeans as his mouth watered for a taste of them.

Reaching out, he allowed the backs of his fingers to smooth over the bared, upper curves.

Her eyes swung back to him, wide, filled with fear and heat.

"Your nipples always get hard when you're kidnapped?" He tried to joke it away, but the tight little buds were just below his fingertips, more tempting than he could have imagined.

She was breathing harder now, her gaze distressed, her cheeks flushed as she shook her head demandingly.

"No?"

The elasticized neckline gave easily to his fingers as they smoothed over the hard curves. They were flushed too, the dark pink nipples standing hard and to attention as the fabric rasped over them.

Oh man, he was going to go to hell for this one for sure.

The elastic hooked beneath the firm mounds, lifting them higher, causing her sweet little nipples to point straight to the ceiling. The hard points were surprisingly engorged, aroused. This wasn't fear. This was her body demanding relief.

Calling himself seven different kinds of a fool, he let his fingers trace a path to one hard little point before his thumb and forefinger gripped one of the hard berries, tugging at firmly, watching her closely.

He didn't expect the reaction. She bucked, her body bowing as the sexual flinch convulsed her petite frame.

"Damn." He was on fire now, almost shaking as a broken little moan tore past the gag and his head lowered.

Helpless mounting lust was riding him so hard, so fast, that he felt drugged, out of control in the face of it. His mouth opened as he covered a trembling peak, drawing it in, sucking it fiercely into his mouth as he leaned over her. His tongue curled around it as she bucked against him, lifting closer, shoving her nipple tight and hard against his tongue as he began to feast.

Chapter Five

∞

This wasn't real. Amanda thrashed beneath the liquid fire of the stranger's mouth. A stranger. Oh God, she wasn't doing this for a stranger, straining closer, trying to shove her breast deeper into his suckling mouth while his tongue wrapped around her nipple like wet velvet.

She wasn't moaning, desperate. Where had that fire come from? The one streaking from her nipple to her womb, convulsing her stomach in spasms of unending, agonizing arousal. And she wasn't panting. She wasn't.

But she was.

She screamed behind the gag, her hands curling into fists as his teeth gripped her nipple, nipping and tugging at it as a flashpoint of wet electricity sizzled between her thighs.

His lips, teeth and tongue worked the point until it was so sensitive she couldn't think of anything but more. She needed more. Needed him sucking it in deep and hard, his teeth sending that curious blend of pleasure and pain streaking to the depths of her pussy as her clit began to swell and beg for attention.

"God, you taste good," he muttered a second before he drew the little point in deep and hard, sucking her into his mouth as a blast of brutal sensation ripped through her.

She twisted beneath him, her hips rising as he leaned over her, desperate growling whimpers escaping the gag as his fingers began to toy with the other nipple. It wasn't enough. Her muffled scream as her body demanded more, shocked her to her core but it didn't ease the horrible, mindless pleasure tearing through it.

Then his fingers tugged harder, the grip becoming tighter as his teeth rasped the other point. Oh God, it hurt with a pleasure she knew would make her insane. She wanted more, needed more. Just a little bit more and the heavy, tormenting pressure just behind her clit would release, easing the liquid fire spilling from her pussy.

"Shit. You like that, don't you?" He raised his head, his eyes narrowed on her as his fingers twisted the nipple it tormented.

She screamed for him, her head pressing back into the mattress as she fought the overwhelming cascade of brutal pleasure.

More.

She needed more.

She couldn't stand the building pressure, the incredible sexual hunger that seemed to rise from a dark, hidden part of her soul. Hunger was like a living being, gnawing at the very depths of her pussy and sending flames to sear the throbbing bud of her clit.

More... She screamed the word behind the gag as he stared down at her.

Oh God. What was wrong with her? Had that blow to the head flipped a sexual switch she couldn't have known existed?

What had he done to her?

He pulled at her nipples again and her gaze glazed over as she fought for breath.

Yes. Yes. Like that.

A fiery golden rush of sensation permeated her body, tingling over her flesh, electrifying her.

"Damn." He was breathing hard too.

His black eyes were bottomless pits of aroused lust, his dark cheekbones flushed, his lips pulled into a tight line of control as she writhed beneath the pressure.

"What do you want, baby?" he whispered then, a wicked sexuality suffusing his expression, giving him a dangerous, dark look.

She arched to him, gasping as his fingers tugged at her nipples again. She wanted his mouth there again. Wanted to feel his lips and teeth tugging at them, drawing on her, making those little streaks of pleasure pain tighten in her womb.

She wanted to know his name.

His head lowered again, and she didn't give a damn what his name was. His mouth was fiery, his tongue an instrument of torture as it rasped and lashed at the peaked flesh and sent her senses careening with pleasure.

Then his teeth nipped at it, sending fiery shards of painful pleasure exploding into her womb.

Her head twisted on the bed, her arms and legs straining against the restraints, her clit was a tortured mass of nerves so in need of relief that all she could think about was the building ache.

"Son of a bitch." He was breathing hard and rough as his head raised, his tongue licking over his already damp lips as the cool air of the room peaked her nipples further.

Please. She wanted to scream the word.

"Damn." He untied the gag quickly, but before she could beg, his lips were covering hers again, his tongue forging into her mouth.

That taste. Honey and spice. Her tongue twined with his, her lips snuggled around it as she sucked it into her mouth, feeling the taste intensify as his hands gripped her head, holding her to him, using his tongue to fuck her mouth with hot, possessive strokes.

His shirt rasped her nipples as he leaned over her, touching her nowhere else, making her crazy for more. She needed more. She whimpered against the need, thrashing against the bed as desperate mewling moans tore from her throat.

When he raised his head, she stared up at him imploringly.

"Make it stop," she gasped. "Please make it stop."

"What?" He was panting as he watched her, his gaze centered on her lips. "Make what stop?"

She whimpered. Why did he want to torture her? What had she done to him?

"Please," she whispered, tears filling her eyes as her clit bloomed into a fiery knot of agony. "It hurts. Make it stop hurting."

He shook his head as though confused. "What hurts?"

Didn't he know? He had turned her into a mass of hunger so intense she was dying with it.

"Damn you," she cursed him bitterly, arching to him, rubbing her breasts into his chest, moaning at the sensation. "You know what I mean. Make it stop now, I can't stand it."

His hand moved from her head, flattening on her waist before smoothing to her thigh. She stilled, her lips parting as she gasped for air, her gaze locked with his as he began to draw the loose skirt of her dress up her legs.

Yes.

Cool air whispered over the stockings she wore, easing the brutal heat for just a second before it returned full force. She twisted as it cleared her knees, arched as the fabric slid over her thighs.

She would have screamed when his fingers grazed the crotch of her panties if his lips hadn't covered hers again, his tongue pumping into her mouth as he suddenly ripped the panties, miniscule as they were, from her writhing body.

When his hand returned, she stilled, a cry tearing from her throat as the heat of his palm cupping her pussy sent arcs of lightning flaring through her body. His head lifted slowly, his eyes narrowed on her, watching her carefully as he moved lower on the bed, pushing her dress to her hips as his eyes went between her thighs.

"Waxed pussy," he whispered. "Do you know what a turn-on that is?"

It was convenient for her. A sense of freedom, a feminine thrill. Now, the sexuality of it ripped through her.

"What have you done to me?" She tried to talk, but it interfered with breathing. She really needed to breathe right now.

"I know what I'm going to do to you," he muttered as his fingers parted the saturated folds, sending fingers of electricity surging over her nerve endings.

Her clit kicked into high gear, the throbbing heat washed over her, causing her to arch, to twist her hips.

"Stay still." The order was followed by a small, stinging slap landing on her cunt.

"Oh God..." Her eyes flew open as she bucked against the fire that ripped through her.

No. No. No. She was screaming the denial in her head, but her clit tightened, her juices flowing from her pussy as the sexual pain nearly pushed her into orgasm. An orgasm she knew would defy all the laws of release and satisfaction that she had so far experienced.

"This is bad," she heard him mutter as he jerked his shirt over his head and stood to the side of the bed.

Tanned and rippling with muscle, his biceps, chest and tightly packed abs were revealed in the low light of the room. Below...she swallowed tightly at the sight of the bulge beneath those jeans.

Broad, strong hands moved to the waistband of his jeans, flicking the snap loose, rasping the zipper down and then pushing the offending material, along with his underwear, down well-muscled legs.

She was sure those legs looked really nice, but who the hell cared. Her eyes centered on the erection straining from between his thighs, hanging low, the heavy weight of the thick muscle pulling it down until it stood out straight from his body.

She swallowed tightly, wondering if there was a chance in hell she could actually accommodate that cock.

"I don't know you," she whispered, licking her lips, knowing it really didn't matter.

"You will soon," he growled.

Before she could say anything more he moved between her thighs, stretching out, his head poised above the wet, throbbing folds of her pussy.

She shuddered in desperation as she felt his breath send a cooling caress over the sensitive tissue.

"Damn, this has to be the prettiest little pussy I've ever laid my eyes on," he whispered, his fingers running through her slit, sending her in to a quaking, shuddering response that tore a cry from her lips. "I'm going to eat you up, baby."

Chapter Six

ॐ

Amanda was certain she died when his tongue followed the path of his fingers. Slowly, languorously his tongue worked the snug little valley, gathering the juices that had pooled along it as she bucked at his lips.

His hands held her hips tight as he licked through folds of flesh that had never known a man's touch.

Reality receded, she no longer cared who he was, what his name was, or what he intended to do with her after he was finished. All she knew was the blistering need slamming through her system, and his hot tongue licking over her flesh like fire.

He moaned into her pussy, licked and sucked at the smooth folds of flesh, then his tongue moved higher, finally, oh dear God, finally rasping over her burning clit.

"Yes," she moaned deliriously. "Oh yes, please, please…"

He growled, a low animalistic sound as his tongue circled the tight little bud, torturing her with her need for release, swamping her with a pleasure so brutal she could barely make sense of what was going on.

"Like that?" he whispered, his breath blowing over the straining mass of nerves.

"Yes." She needed more, needed him closer.

"You taste perfect," he growled. "Like hot honey syrup, smooth and sweet on my tongue."

She whimpered, her head twisting on the bed as she fought the need to beg for more.

"Do you want to come, baby?" he asked, his voice wickedly teasing. "Your little clit is so hard and swollen. Do you want me to make it feel better?"

"Yes," she cried. "Do you want me to beg?"

"Oh yeah," he laughed, a low dark sound. "Tell me what you want, sweetheart. Beg me to make you come."

She was beyond shame. Beyond the normal boundaries of virgin hesitance.

"Suck it," she begged, "suck my clit. Hard. Do it hard. Like you did my nipples."

"Mmm." The vibration of pleasure as he licked through the burning slit nearly sent her over the edge.

"Do you like it when I hurt you?" he asked her. "When I pinched your little nipples and tugged at them with them my teeth?"

"Oh God." She shook like a leaf in a hurricane. "Yes. I do. Please, please do something."

His fingers slid through her juices, moving down, caressing over the entrance to her vagina before circling the little puckered hole of her rear. She jerked at the caress but lay still, shaking as he did it again, then again. The fourth time she choked on a cry as the tip of his finger slid into her.

Fire. Heat.

He gathered more of her juices and repeated the movement, over and over again as his tongue licked at her swollen pussy, until she screamed with the building pressure when his finger slid deep, deep inside her burning rear.

His lips clamped on her clit then, his tongue rasping it as he sucked it into his mouth. His finger moved inside her, fucking into the untouched channel and sending those much needed, hungry flames burning through her body.

So close. She was so close... Another finger joined the first then, working into her, stretching her, burning her as his mouth suckled her, his tongue flicking pressing, destroying her.

When her climax hit, she screamed. She couldn't stop the sound, couldn't control the response. Fire was streaking through her ass, burning her alive with the pleasure and the pain as she exploded with such force, such overwhelming response, that nothing mattered, nothing existed but the conflagration tightening her body and burning her alive.

Until... "Hell, Kiowa, you were supposed to protect her, not fuck her."

What happened next was little more than a hazy realization of a blanket being jerked over her as—Kiowa?—came over her with a gun aimed at the door and a growl that sounded all too animal-like.

"Damn, Simon, forget the gun in his hand, look at that dick!" the female who had entered crooned with husky appreciation.

Kiowa growled again, frustration eating him alive as Stephanie's dark, wide eyes centered between his body where he crouched over Amanda.

The slender, pretty, female mercenary stood beside her much taller lover, Simon Quatres, who grimaced with male distaste.

"Down, girl," he muttered, before giving a Kiowa a hard look. "Could you put some pants on or something?"

He could still smell Amanda's arousal, sweet and hot. Beneath him, she stared back at Simon and Stephanie in dazed fascination, though he could feel the fine shudders working through her body as he tasted the essence of her need on his lips. And he wanted more.

Cursing he jumped from the bed and dragged his jeans over his hips before struggling to pull the zipper over an erection that howled in discontent at the confinement.

"Your timing sucks, Simon," he snapped when he turned back to them, but his gaze went to Amanda.

She was staring up at him, dazed, almost drugged. But there had been no signs of drugs, he would have sensed it first thing. He frowned, moving closer to check her dilated pupils and feel the warmth of her skin.

Her whispered moan as he touched her had his senses screaming in demand. She needed to be fucked. He could smell it on the air around her, taste it on his lips, feel it surging like a wave of heat around him.

And he wanted to fuck her, so damned bad it made his back teeth hurt.

"You know, for a damned careful man, you're making some major mistakes here," Simon said then. "Did you forget who she was by chance? Maybe her would-be attackers hit you on the head or something?"

Simon's blue eyes regarded him with sharp disapproval.

"I didn't forget who she was," he snarled back. "Let it alone and tell me what the hell happened to her Secret Service detail."

Simon grunted. "Strange thing going on there, buddy," he said sarcastically. "Gloria and the Ladies showed up at her place. No dead bad guys and the Goof Troup was in place next door safe and sound. All we found was a little blood on the back walk and it looked like several other patches of it had been carefully erased. Someone was busy."

Someone was playing games.

Kiowa breathed in deeply, fighting to ignore the smell of hot willing flesh just behind him. Dammit, it wasn't like he did without sex. He shouldn't be so fucking aroused, so hungry to devour that sweet little body laid out like a pasha's favorite toy.

"Any ideas?" he asked Simon then.

Simon shrugged, his shoulders flexing beneath the dark T-shirt he wore as he glanced at Amanda again.

"Word reached me there was a hit planned. Just as Dash told you. The blood supremacists have plans to use her to influence the vote next week on Breed Law. Somehow, they must have found a way to keep her disappearance from leaking to the general public. Though how they intended to do that I have no clue. Someone real close to President Marion would have to be involved in it."

The other man's eyes flickered to the bed behind Kiowa again. Turning, Kiowa wished he had stayed put. She was shifting beneath the blankets, a low, weak moan filling the air.

"Did you drug her?" Simon's tone was suspicious as he watched the girl.

"No, and they didn't either." He pushed his fingers through his long black hair and fought to get a handle on his hunger. "Damned if know what happened. They hit her on the head, but if she was drugged, I can't sense it."

And Kiowa was damned good at sensing drugs.

"She's not exactly aware." Stephanie stepped closer to the bed, a frown marking her dark brow. "If I didn't know better, I'd say she had a dose of Rohypnol."

Kiowa ground his teeth together furiously. "You think I need to pump someone full of date rape drugs to get fucked, Steph?"

Her eyes widened innocently. "With that dick? Duh. I'm certain of it. But I was accusing them more than you."

"I know what that shit smells like." He grimaced. He knew only too well. "She's not drugged."

Simon moved to the bed while Kiowa felt every muscle in his body tense in objection to the other man going anywhere near her.

She shifted on the bed again, the blanket moving with her splayed, bound legs as her breasts heaved beneath it. He tightened his jaw, gritting his teeth as another wave of heat washed over him.

Simon reached for the blanket.

The warning growl that came from Kiowa's throat was accompanied by a snarl. He knew what the others saw. Curved canines flashing at the side of his mouth as he moved quickly to push Simon out of the way.

"Don't fucking touch her." The low, rumbling sound of his voice shocked him as much as it did Simon.

"This is a problem, Kiowa." He frowned then, his blue eyes flashing in anger. "If she dies, we're up shit creek."

"She's not going to die," he snapped, certain of that fact.

"Kiowa, pay attention here," Simon spoke with sarcastic patience. "You're not a stupid man. Look at her. Something is fucking wrong with her."

"Goddammit I know that," he shot back, frustration eating at him. "The same fucking thing is wrong with me, now get the hell off my back."

He paced to the end of the bed. Bad idea. The smell of her arousal was like a punch to his gut. Something was wrong, and damned if it wasn't killing him too.

"Call him." He turned on Simon again. "Now!"

Simon's eyes widened. "Man, you don't just call him. He calls you."

She moaned again, a low distressed sound that twisted his gut and made his cock jerked in demand.

"Simon, you have three seconds to call him," he snarled. "After that I'm going to rip your fucking head off your shoulders and jerk your guts out your throat. And I can do it."

He was one of the few men that would try.

"You're gonna get my ass kicked," Simon snarled.

"Better kicked than dead," Kiowa retorted. "Don't push me Simon. I want to talk to him now."

Simon jerked the cell phone from its hip holder and punched a button furiously before handing the phone to Kiowa.

"What?" The voice at the other end was wary, careful.

"We have a problem," Kiowa reported, his patience straining to the limit as he listened to a series of pauses and low clicks that indicated added security to the line.

"What's the problem?" Dash Sinclair wasn't known for his friendly personality or his patience with problems. His military training and danger surrounding him and his family made for one very suspicious man.

"Babysitting duty has gone sour," he snapped tightly. "She was hit on the head but woke up fine. Now, she's showing all the signs of date rape drugs with none of the drug in her system. She's in distress..." Damn, so was he. He was about to come in his jeans with each little whimpering moan from her throat.

"Shit!" The sizzling curse that came across the line surprised him. Dash didn't upset easily. "Did you kiss her?"

Kiss her?

"What the fuck does that have to do with anything?"

"Listen to me, you mangy asshole," Dash snapped, causing Kiowa to grimace at the insult. "Did you or did you not kiss her?"

"Yes," he snarled back. "She was getting ready to scream, I kissed her. Now what the hell does that have to do with shit?"

"God, if Callan doesn't lift the restriction on this information someone is going to get killed," Dash muttered. "Listen to me Kiowa; you have a shit load of problems here."

"It was a kiss," he bit out. "Do you think I've never kissed a woman before? It never hurt one before."

"You weren't kissing your fucking mate before either," Dash snarled, causing Kiowa to still in shock. "Is your tongue swollen?"

Swollen? It was throbbing as hard as his dick was.

"Kiowa?" Dash snapped seconds later. "Answer me."

"Yes, Sir," he replied without thinking, the military tone Dash used snapping into his brain when nothing else could.

"Damn."

"What?" Kiowa snarled. "Explain it."

"No time and not enough security," Dash informed him, his voice turning cold. "Hold on."

Hold on? Amanda arched beneath the blanket again, her head twisting on the mattress as she whimpered heatedly. The smell of her juices had his body on fire, his mouth watering for the taste of her sweet little pussy.

His hand clenched the phone as he fought the need to push Simon and Steph from the room. If he didn't get his cock in her soon he was going to go insane.

"No extraction available," Dash suddenly snapped. "Proceed to Alpha location and await further information."

Kiowa snorted. That was just his luck, no way to get a helicopter to him and now Dash was sending him to the one place guaranteed to get him killed.

"Yeah, right, Major," he growled. "Like I can get in there."

"Clearance has been arranged and explanations will be given. In the meantime, don't kiss her again, and do nothing to heighten her arousal. Get your ass there now, Kiowa, and hers. You don't have time to spare. Now let me talk to Simon."

He handed the phone to the other man as he moved to release the ties that bound Amanda's slender ankles. The three-inch heels on the leather ankle boots were so damned sexy he wanted to howl at the sight of it. And those red stockings were enough to make a man come in his jeans.

Leaving the blanket on her, he ignored Simon's part of the conversation as well as the extra call he made seconds later. Kiowa untied Amanda's hands instead, massaging the fragile wrists as she turned to him.

"I'm cold," she whispered, lifting drowsy eyes to his.

"I know, baby." He kept his voice soft, as gentle as possible as he discreetly straightened her clothes and wrapped her snuggly in the blanket.

She didn't smell cold though. She smelled hot and sweet and ready to take every inch of his throbbing cock.

"Tell me what's wrong with me." Her voice was slurred, her eyes so dilated that only a fragile ring of color remained.

"You're going to be fine, baby," he whispered against her forehead, laying a kiss on the damp flesh as she trembled in his arms.

"We have a Grand Cherokee outside," Simon reported as he hung the phone up. The two of you can lie in the back. I'll drive. Keep her down, yourself as well. We'll arrive at Alpha location early morning."

Kiowa glanced at the clock. It was barely ten, would he last that long?

"Steph, go outside and watch the area. We have to load her up and get the hell out of here before anyone tracking can find us. Gloria and the others will ride shotgun. Let's head out."

The backseat in the Grand Cherokee had been lowered, the vehicle backed close to the door with the back door swung open. Kiowa carried his hot little burden out the door and finally managed to wedge his long frame in beside hers.

Pillows from the motel bed cushioned their heads as the back was closed and Simon and Steph jumped into the front. It wasn't a pillow Amanda Lee Marion wanted though.

She curled against Kiowa's chest, the blanket covering her falling away enough to allow her to press one swollen hard-tipped breast into his chest.

"How far is the fucking compound from here?" he growled as he glanced at Simon between the seats.

The other man was trying really hard not to laugh. Kiowa made a mental note to kick his ass when the hard-on went down enough to allow for it.

"Almost six hours," Stephanie answered him quietly. "We're taking back roads more than interstate just in case. So far, nothing has been reported on her abduction or any sign that anyone knows anything is awry. With any luck, we'll reach Virginia without problem."

No problems for her maybe.

Kiowa couldn't stop himself from holding Amanda closer as she pressed into him, her leg lifting to hug his close, pressing his thigh against her wet pussy. And she was wet. God, she was so wet he just wanted to go between her thighs and drown in her.

Another soft little moan left her throat as he helplessly pressed harder against her, rasping her straining clit with his thigh as she arched in his arms.

"Turn the fucking radio on, Quatres," he snarled, holding her head close, furious that the other man would hear those unbidden, soft little moans.

"No kissing, Kiowa," Simon reminded him sternly as he flipped the radio on and the soft, haunting sounds filled the Jeep. "And no touching."

Fuck it. He could touch all the hell he wanted. She was sliding against his body like silk and satin and he would be damned if he could keep his hands to himself. But he did want that kiss.

His tongue was tight and swollen, small glands at the side of it throbbing almost painfully. This was damned strange. Sex had never been like this, nor had arousal.

His mate. Dash Sinclair's words rolled over him as Amanda's soft little hands kneaded his chest. She was his mate?

Coyotes weren't supposed to have loyalty or emotions, let alone mates. Somehow, a few of them had been lucky enough to know loyalty, to create friends and keep them. Some, like Kiowa, had been raised outside the prisons, but the life he had led himself hadn't exactly inspired the need for loyalties, though he had made a few.

His hand smoothed down her back, his fingers clenching in the full curve of her buttock as her hot little lips found his nipple beneath his shirt.

His teeth clenched as a hard breath escaped his throat. Fuck. Her teeth were working him with exquisite heat, her tongue stroking over the fabric of the shirt as her hands moved sluggishly to press beneath the bottom of the material.

He threw his head back, closed his eyes and fought the need. A need so intense, so all-consuming he doubted he would make it an hour, let alone six.

Chapter Seven

ຂ

What was wrong with her? Amanda knew something was horribly wrong, that the heat and hunger that kept her body so sensitized and filled with a painful arousal wasn't natural.

It happened with that kiss. She remembered the kiss. The stranger, Kiowa, locking his lips to hers and spreading the taste of sweet honey through her senses. That was when it happened. Within seconds, heat had filled her, making it hard to think, to make sense of anything but the pleasure and the need for his touch.

And touch her he had. She moved against him now, remembering his lips on her breasts, his teeth at her nipple, sending sizzling bolts of exquisite pleasure pain tearing through her.

She had known for years that regular, normal sex would never be enough for her. The staid kisses and boring touches she had received over the years had been less than enjoyable. But, when she touched herself, her fingers pinching at her nipples, stroking her clit with a harder touch, there she had found pleasure.

The books she hid and read, sizzling romances that involved just a bit of the more painful love play, would keep her hot and wet for days. But never hot enough for this. To accept the kiss, the touch of a man she didn't even know.

She shuddered as she remembered his hand slapping her cunt, the vibrations of heat and mild pain streaking into her clit and nearly sending her senses spinning. She wanted more of it. Wanted to feel his hand there again, making her burn, making her twist against him as the pleasure ripped her apart.

God, this was so wrong. She shouldn't be like this. Had he drugged her? She didn't remember it if he had. And she didn't feel drugged exactly; it's just that all her senses were centered on one thing and one thing only. His touch.

"Easy, baby," he groaned at her ear as her teeth teased his nipple.

Her hand slipped beneath his shirt as she gasped at the heat of his hard body and felt his straining erection pressing against her through the rough jeans. That's what she wanted, his cock pressing into her, stilling the heat throbbing in her pussy.

Her hands drifted down, plucking at the snap as his breathing escalated. She just wanted to touch him, wanted to wiggle down until she could take it in her mouth, lick it and suck it as she had read about. She wanted it. God now, she had to have it.

Her hands were tearing at his jeans, desperate whimpers coming from her throat as his hands covered hers, dragging them back to his chest.

"Amanda, listen to me," he crooned at her ear. "Listen to me very carefully, baby. You have to stop. Lie still and sweet against me just for a little bit longer."

Like hell. He had kidnapped her. He had taken her from her home for only God knew what reason, and chances were good he would kill her before it was over it. But before he did he was going to still the fever raging in her body or she would kill him first.

"Kiss me," she whispered, her head falling back, staring up at him in dazed wonder.

He was so good-looking. Native American features, black, black eyes, long black hair that spilled over the side of his neck as he watched her with hungry intent. He didn't look like a man willing to kill. Those weren't the cold blue eyes that stared at her from behind a mask, and his voice wasn't filled with hatred.

"Ah sweetheart, that's what has us in this mess now," he growled, his hand tightening at her buttock, pulling at the flesh.

The action sent a strange, tightening sensation through her anus. She flushed as she remembered his fingers there, spearing into her, opening her as his mouth ate at her clit, sucking her in and sending her flying. She wanted it again.

"You did this," she groaned, aching so bad she wondered if she would survive it. "You did this to me. Now fix it."

A rumbled growl vibrated in his chest.

"Soon."

"Now."

A rough chuckle, almost pain-filled, washed over her senses.

"We have company, baby. You want me to make you scream in front of them?"

"I don't care." And she didn't. All of fucking Washington D.C. could be looking on at that moment and she wouldn't care. "Kiss me."

She needed his taste again.

She wiggled her hands from beneath his then, one moving to cup the hard erection as he stiffened, a hiss echoing in her ear. The other worked at his jeans again.

Her friend, Beth, had swore that all you had to do was touch their cocks and they were putty in your hands. Was it true?

The snap came undone, the zipper rasped down, and suddenly her hands were filled with steel-hard, iron-hot male cock.

"Damn it to hell," he cursed roughly, his big body trembling as she wrapped both hands around impossibly thick flesh.

The head was flared, the shaft roughly ridged as blood pulsed just beneath the flesh. Her mouth watered. She wanted to taste him, make him as crazy with her mouth as he made her with his.

"Simon, goddammit, I'm not going to last like this."

His rough curse was ignored. He wasn't saying her name, so what the hell did she care? She tried to wiggle down further, whimpering as his hard hands held her in place.

"Five more hours, Kiowa."

Five hours? The comment had laughter rippling through her mind. If anyone thought she was going to wait five hours and suffer through this agony of arousal, they were crazier than hell.

"Kiss me," she whispered again, staring up at him in the dim light of the vehicle they were obviously traveling in. "Kiss me or let me touch you. Please."

His expression was tortured.

"Don't you do it, Kiowa. Dammit, we don't have time to stop for this shit."

She wished that voice would just shut the hell up.

She licked her lips slowly.

"I need you. It hurts, Kiowa."

His name whispering from her lips was the trigger. She gave herself a mental high five as a rough groan shuddered from him and his head lowered.

There was the taste, the heat she needed. Amanda opened her lips for his tongue, clamping down on it and suckling eagerly as it filled her mouth. She twisted against him, feeling his cock throb harder in her hand as he began to move over her body.

He laid her flat, coming over her as his big hand pushed the bodice of her gown down, his fingers gripping her nipple as he pumped his tongue in her mouth. Her hands lost contact with his erection, but that was okay, she needed his shoulders to hold onto as the pain and the pleasure began to whip through her nervous system.

The heat built higher, hotter. Her nipple, inflamed and begging for more, throbbed between his fingers as he tugged at it, his fingers pressing into it and making lightning sear her clit.

His knee pressed hers apart as his thigh shoved against her pussy, making her gasp as it ground into her clit. Sweet mercy, yes. She wanted to scream with the pleasure, but his mouth covered hers, his tongue filling her, stroking her, making her twist and shudder beneath him as the pleasure tore through her.

"Goddammit, Simon." He jerked his head back, holding her close again as he fought for air, his grip on her nipple making her whimper.

God, it was so good. She wanted his mouth there, his teeth, the wet heat searing her from the inside out.

An argument ensued. She really didn't care what it was over. Her lips were busy at his neck, his chest, moving down, her hunger for his cock driving her past sanity. She had always thought she would love giving head. Reading about it had made her mouth water, the thought of being held, hard hands tangled in her hair as they were now, forcing her mouth to fill with steel-hard male flesh, feeling it fuck between her lips as harsh male groans echoed in her ears.

She reach the damp crest, her tongue swiping over it eagerly as he suddenly stilled and the vehicle came to a rocking stop. Car doors slammed, then the blanket was jerked from her as both hands held her head as the thick hot flesh speared between her lips.

Chapter Eight

ॐ

"Fuck yes!" Kiowa was in heaven. Or hell. He wasn't certain which yet, but he knew for damned sure that kissing the hot little package whose mouth was currently filled with his dick, hadn't been his brightest moment.

He leaned back, panting as he watched several inches of his thick erection stretch that sweet rosebud mouth. The light of the moon speared into the vehicle, his own eyesight perfect, enhancing the sight.

Her tongue was swirling around the head, her mouth sucking at him desperately. He was going to fuck her. He knew he was. He was going to spread those pretty thighs and watch every inch of his flesh disappear inside her pretty cunt. He was going to have to do it soon before he was going to spill his pleasure in her mouth instead.

Would it matter? He groaned at the thought.

"Suck it, baby." He pulled her hair, because he knew she liked the pain.

He was rewarded by another inch disappearing into her mouth as he felt a hard pulse of semen—although it didn't feel like semen—gush into her mouth.

What was that? The pleasure from it stripped his control, almost like getting off just enough for relief, but this time, there was no relief, the hunger burned brighter, hotter instead.

The taste must have pleased her. She took another inch, her lips flattening, her tongue like liquid fire as it stroked the sensitive little spot just beneath the tapered crest.

"Damn, your mouth is hot. Hot and sweet. Suck that cock, baby. Show me how much you need it, how much you want it."

Another hot spurt of fluid and she was devouring him. Her mouth was working on him with wet precision, drawing his balls up to the base of his erection as he gritted his teeth and fought the impending explosion.

He didn't want to rush this. Didn't want it to end. Not yet. It was too hot, too much pleasure, more than he had ever known in his life. Her mouth moved on his so sweetly, snug and tight, her tongue licking him like a favorite treat as his hands kneaded her hair firmly.

Oh, she liked that. She whimpered around his dick, one hand tightening on the base of this erection as the fingers of the other pricked at the flesh of his thigh.

He had never been a gentle man, not in his dealings with others or sexually. He was what he was, simple, basic. He spoke when he needed to, did his job the best he could and fucked for the sheer pleasure of it. He had never taken a woman who didn't know exactly what she was doing and he had never lost control with one.

He was on the verge of losing control with this one.

"Enough." He had to force himself to raise her head, grimacing in pleasure at the sound of the little pop his cock made as it exited her mouth.

"I want more," she moaned, struggling against him as he jerked the blanket further away from her.

"Later." He wanted her. The smell of her heat was killing him, addictive, consuming.

His lips moved to one hard nipple as he groaned when she pushed it deep in his mouth. She knew what she wanted.

"Bite me." Her request had his blood pressure soaring.

He gripped the hard tip of her nipple between his teeth, allowing them to pinch and sensitize the little nubbin as her cries echoed around him.

Had another woman ever asked him to bite her? Had another ever relished that fine line of pleasure and pain in such a way?

"Like that?" he growled, lifting from her as hands worked at the metal clasps of the bodice before tearing it from her body.

The dress was easy. He ripped it off her. There was no time to be nice, no time to care about the decency of the act. He wanted her naked. Now.

Moonlight glossed her slender body, her rounded little belly, caused her honeyed pussy to glisten as he moved her to the center of the area and spread her legs wide.

"Damn, you're so small," he whispered, toeing off his moccasins before struggling out his jeans.

Finally, he was naked, as bare as she was, staring at the banquet laid out before him. She lifted to him, the sweet folds of her cunt shining wetly in the dim light.

Then he touched her. His fingers parted her, sliding through the shallow slit before circling her clit. Watching her through narrowed eyes, he lifted his hand then before delivering a light little slap to the swollen pad.

She cried out harshly, arching her hips as the scent of sweet hot woman filled the interior of the SUV.

"Play with your nipples," he ordered her then, moving her hands to her breasts. "Pinch them. Pull at them. Show me how you like it."

His cock was ready to explode. Her slender fingers gripped the berry ripe points, exerting more pressure than he would have, pulling at the distending buds as she gasped in pleasure.

He slapped her pussy again, using enough force to make the little blow warm her flesh.

"Yes. Oh yes..." She was panting, sweat glistening on her body as her legs spread wider.

Her clit was fully distended, peeking past the swollen lips and glistening with her cream.

God, the things he could do to her. The ways he could take her and make her love it. He wouldn't have to hold back with her as he had other women. She rose to the little love pain, shaking and begging for more. Her eyes glittered in the darkness, her pale body shuddering in arousal.

He slickened his fingers again, testing the wash of juices from her pussy as he moved closer.

"It's going to hurt," he promised her. "Is that what you want, Manda? Are you sure?"

Amanda shook beneath the hard stare, so aroused now, pushed so far past reality that she just didn't give a damn. She was dying in need, the curling, agonizing hunger worse than anything she had known in her life.

Her eyes went to his straining cock, certain her dazed senses were seeing more than was really there.

"I want it," she whispered, her juices flooding her cunt at the thought of it. "Now. I want it now."

He came over her slowly, his big body dwarfing hers, his muscles rippling in the moonlight as she felt the broad head of his cock nudge at her hungry cunt. And it was thick. Wide.

She whimpered in anticipation. She had once heard her brother's wife snickering that wider was better, but she had no idea what she meant until now.

"Hold onto me," he whispered then, moving her hands from her breasts to his shoulders. "It won't be easy, Manda."

She loved how he said her name.

Her hands gripped his shoulders as she felt his cock press deeper. Then she felt it spurt, just as it had in her mouth. She moaned at the delicious burn that filled her. Then her eyes widened as he pressed deeper, another spurt filling her, making her shake with the combination of sensations. She could feel her pussy relaxing, yet the arousal was building.

Oh God, he was starting to fill her. She writhed beneath him as he leaned back, his eyes going to where their bodies were slowly connecting. He held her hips elevated, his hands lifting her to him as he forged in further. Another hard spurt, a burning insidious pleasure that had her screaming his name.

Could she bear it? He was stretching her, pushing apart muscle and tissue that had never known another's touch but her own. She could feel her pussy protesting, tightening to grip the wide head as it began to forge inside her.

"Fuck. You're tight." His voice was a rough, almost inhuman growl. "Relax, baby. Relax for me, just a little bit."

She tightened further and his eyes narrowed on her.

"I'll make you scream," he warned her then. "It could hurt more than you're counting on, sweetheart."

She milked him, rippling the overstretched flesh that encased only a portion of the crest.

His hands tightened, his thighs bunched beneath hers and then she felt the breath slamming from her body as he drove the head, only the head, inside her. He was working it there then. Short little strokes that caressed her burning cunt and had her shaking beneath him.

"More." She could barely breathe, let alone talk.

All she could do was feel. The burning pressure, the agonizing ache for more.

"Fuck." He stopped then, shuddering. "Dammit it, Manda. Goddammit, you're a fucking virgin." He sounded tortured.

She tightened on him, staring up at him imploringly.

"More."

He threw his head back, obviously fighting for control.

"Kiowa. Fuck me," she cried, her voice ragged now. "I can't stand it. Fill me, Kiowa…"

She screamed until she was certain her voice would break. He came over her, holding her in place a second before he thrust inside her, hard and heavy. Her juices were thick, slick, aiding the penetration as he split through the unused channel, burying inside her to the hilt in one sure thrust.

She bucked in his arms, her nails digging into his shoulders as his lips moved at her neck, curses and whispered apologies caressing her ear as he began to move. Lightning was blazing through her body, hard, explosive streaks of fire burning her, driving her higher as the pleasure and the pain combined, making her convulse in his arms as she fought for orgasm.

There was no control left for either of them. He was fucking into her, hard deep lunges that had her crying out his name as she felt each hard thrust stretching her, caressing her. He shafted her with quick long strokes that stole her breath and had her senses rioting and drove her closer and closer to the brink.

Where she needed to be.

"Kiowa..." She was screaming his name again as she felt it building in her. A conflagration in the center of her womb, tightening, building...

When it burst through her, only madness reigned. She felt herself stretching, stretching, hot pulses of fire erupting in her pussy as sharp teeth locked on her shoulder, piercing the flesh.

Her eyes opened wide, staring sightlessly upward as she felt the swelling in the cock now locked deep inside her, spurting pulse after pulse of semen deep inside her womb.

She wasn't stupid. What she was feeling was much too similar to the joking references to the Wolf Breeds. They were created from wolf DNA. "Do their cocks knot?" one teacher had asked with an exaggerated shiver of delight.

Knotted. She shuddered again before realization slammed into her, shockingly cold as her eyes met his. She shuddered in his grip, the fear, the hunger, the insane desire for more rising within her, locking her mind into one thought alone.

"Animal..." The thought wrenched through her body, spilled from her lips as shock rocked her very foundations. The pleasure was twisting, ripping through her, taking her breath, her will, her mind.

Regret twisted his expression and seared her soul as his head lowered, his teeth grazing her neck an instant before he bit into her...

Chapter Nine

ಖ

"Amanda?" Kiowa moved from her slowly, easing his cock from the fist-tight confines of her pussy, a grimace of pleasure twisting his face as her flesh continued to suck at him until he popped free.

She was crying. God help him, what had happened? He hadn't heard of anything this unusual, the animal side of their natures revealing itself in this manner. His hand was trembling as he smoothed the long fall of her hair back from her neck, guilt staining his soul at the mark that now marred the flesh between her shoulder and her neck.

He had bitten her. Ruthlessly, without conscience, he had sunk the curved canines into her flesh and held her still as the engorged knot that locked him inside her held his cock at the mouth of her womb, spurting his semen deep and hard inside the tight channel.

She curled on her side, dragging the blanket with her as her breath hitched tearfully.

"I'm okay." It was obvious she was trying to be brave, trying to fight past the shock and the fear that he could smell emanating from her. She was confused, thrown into something that even he couldn't make enough sense of to help her.

She had been a virgin, untouched, so sensual and naturally erotic she had stolen his breath with each touch, each caress she had begged for so sweetly. And he had done this to her, locked inside her like the animal that howled just beneath the surface.

"That's never happened." He swiped his fingers through his hair as he knelt beside her, frowning at the shudders that

59

racked her body. "Amanda. That's never happened to me before."

"Yes, well. It hasn't happened to me either," she responded tearfully. "God, just go away. I need to think. I need to..." A sob caught in her throat, the smell of her tears sinking into his heart.

He drew in a hard, deep breath.

"I know you're scared." He fought to keep from touching her, to keep from taking her again. "We'll fix this. Somehow."

"How?" She turned back to him again, her eyes blazing, shimmering with tears. "What the hell is wrong with me? This isn't me and it isn't my body. What did you do to me?"

He could hear the rage gathering in her voice now, and he could smell the hunger. His mouth went dry at the scent of female lust, as his tongue tightened, impossibly feeling as though it were swelling within his mouth once again. It had done that before, as his mouth covered hers to keep her from screaming. And it had then dipped into her mouth the taste... The taste had been indescribable.

"I don't know. But whatever it was, it was mutual, Amanda." He wanted to snarl the words in defense, but managed to keep his voice soft, his tone calm.

"Was it?" She moved slowly, sitting up, pulling her legs in close to her body as she stared back at him furiously. "Doesn't any of this seem the least bit odd to you? This isn't natural."

"So you said before." He pushed back the anger at that single word, "animal".

"Did they drug me?" She shook her head in confusion. "The guy who grabbed me hit me, I know that. Did they drug me?"

She was searching desperately for an excuse. One he couldn't give her.

"There were no drugs." He searched the corner of the Jeep for his jeans. "I checked first thing. Whatever happened was natural."

"This isn't natural," she cried out. "I don't act like that. Not with strangers, with…"

"Animals?" He held back the sneer, barely.

"With anyone," she snapped back before shaking her head, the smell of her fear growing stronger. "Take me home. You have to take me back home. Call my father. Now! He'll come after me."

"No!" Possessive rage nearly overwhelmed him before he managed to push it back along with the pain of her rejection. "We're taking you somewhere safe…"

"No! Take me home!"

"No." The growl that vibrated in his voice shocked her to silence as her eyes widened, her lips parting on a gasp. "Not now. Not yet. Not by God until I can get the smell of your hunger from my head."

He didn't understand the rage, the determination to keep her that suddenly welled within him, but he knew if he didn't get away from her, he was going to take her. Over and over again, the smell of her fear mixing with her lust until it drove him insane.

Jerking the door beside him open, he jumped from the Jeep, his jeans forgotten, the chill of the late October air barely noticeable for the heat climbing in his body. A heat he feared he would never be free of. Just as he would never be free of the animal Amanda saw within him.

* * * * *

"Shit's hit the fan, amigo." Simon spoke quietly into the cell phone as Kiowa plunged into the frigid depths of the lake they had parked beside.

Finding the little out-of-the-way place for nature to take its course had been a bitch.

Dash sighed wearily.

"How far are you from Alpha site?"

"Good four and a half hours," he muttered. "We were lucky to get this close. That girl was in sad shape for a while, my friend. Those little moans were killing me. God only knows what it did to him."

There were few people aware of the exact nature of the mating processes in the Breeds. Callan had imposed a strict code of silence on the few Breeds who had mated so far, hoping to secure a safer environment in world opinion before it leaked out.

Simon was the only non-breed with such information. He had it only because he was a sneaky son of a bitch with a sharper mind than most people when it came to animals.

Dash cursed low and viciously.

"Yeah, for all of me too." Simon grimaced. "Our little pup is presently swimming in frigid waters and his sweet thang is huddled in nothing more than a blanket. What do we do?"

"Get them to Alpha Site," Dash snapped. "We're wasting time we fucking don't have, Simon."

"Hey, you're jumping the wrong dude here, asshole," Simon growled. "It's not my dick tied in a knot with a woman hotter than the hounds of hell. Try telling him."

"Try pulling out now," he snapped. "You have escorts in position beginning one hour from your location. Move now, goddammit, no matter what."

"Fuck." Simon snapped the phone closed.

Major Sinclair was going to keep on; he was going to get his ass kicked.

"So?" Stephanie moved closer, wrapping her arms around his waist from behind as she laid her cheek against his back.

"So, we go," he sighed. "Let's hope they got enough, because we gotta trot, baby doll. My guess is, there are hounds baying at our heels and Dash knows it. He was amazingly reserved." He grimaced at the Major's curses. "We have escorts an hour from here, so my guess is Feline Cavalry is moving in as insurance."

"Shit." She pressed her head tighter against his back.

"Yep. That 'bout sums it up," he drawled. "Let's get the kiddies moving and pray we're ahead of the bad guys. I really ain't lookin' to tangle with government firepower here. That would be a bad thing."

A very, very bad thing.

Stephanie moved to his side as Kiowa strode naked from the lake, breathing harshly, but the cold water had no effect on the erection straining from his body.

"Simon honey, that man is packed," Steph remarked with no small amount of feminine interest. "But damned if I think I'd want a piece of it. He looks mean enough to bite."

Simon snorted. Yep. And he was betting a lot of money Kiowa had bit. Very, very bad.

Chapter Ten

ഇ

Stay down. Don't risk being seen. Stay covered.

Definitely stay covered.

Amanda lay on her side, her back to Kiowa as she tried to hug the wheel cover and keep from touching him.

Cold hard reality had almost returned. Enough to realize what had happened and to remember in bleak clarity the hours before when it had all begun. How long had passed? It was nearly three in the morning now, Simon had told Kiowa a bit ago. The lights from the vehicle following them flipped in and out of the back glass, casting odd shadows around her.

Nearly three. It had been just after seven when she had closed her door on the trick-or-treaters. Seven hours. In seven hours her life had changed so drastically she was certain she could never right it again.

She shuddered at the thought of it. Not in distaste. She wished it were in distaste, it would make it easier. It would ease the tears that slid silently down her face and the ache that lay heavy in her heart.

What had she done? How had it happened? And why was she still being tortured with the need for more?

"How much longer, Simon?" Kiowa snapped from beside her, his voice harsh as he demanded the answer.

"A little over an hour," Simon answered back. "Callan has one of the new cabins ready. They're gathering intel now. We should have something when we get there."

"Sinclair there?" His voice was a raspy growl. He was pissed. Good, so was she.

"He's flying in with Elizabeth and Cassie now. He should be there just ahead of us."

She could feel the tension filling the Jeep now. Between her and Kiowa. The more she burned, the madder he seemed to get.

Could he tell? she wondered. Did he sense the building arousal? Just what she needed. The son of a bitch didn't just drug her with some kind of weird animal aphrodisiac, but he could sense the effect of it.

"Dash Sinclair is in on this?" She spoke up then, stilling the tears as anger washed over her.

She had met Dash Sinclair and his wife Elizabeth. Their daughter Cassie was a sweet, if odd little child. They had met with her father during one of the endless meetings the month before.

"None of us were in on anything, Ms. Marion, but protecting your hide," Simon told her harshly. "Things are turning out bad, I admit, but we did our best."

"Your best sucks," she informed him furiously. "They'll find me."

Her father would not take this lying down, she thought. If the Breeds thought they had trouble before, it would be nothing compared to what her father and brother would bring down on them now.

"They have to know you've gone first," Kiowa snapped. "The five men I took out behind your house disappeared, Manda. And they didn't walk away. Your security detail is *still* sleeping peacefully and breathing. For the moment. And your father doesn't have a clue you're gone."

She blinked back at him. She remembered Tammy Brock then, her nervousness, her request to use the bathroom. How had they convinced Tammy to help them? Better yet, why had her bodyguards ignored the back door indicator light as they had? At no time was she supposed to use that door after dark. She never had.

"The security detail was helping them," she whispered in shock. "They had to be. Tammy deactivated the alarm on the back door when she went to the bathroom, but they should have known that. The safeguards would have warned them of that."

"Damn, she's a bright one, Kiowa. You might want to consider keeping her." Simon's glowing praise was slightly mocking.

Bastard.

"Why would they do that?" She shook her head, refusing to turn and even glance at Kiowa. If she looked at him, saw his eyes, his mouth, she would be a goner. "I can almost understand Tammy if it's money. Kylie is so sick. But why did the guards help?"

"Well, that's one we're trying to figure out," Simon answered her. "Who's this Tammy person anyway?"

She quickly explained what had occurred with Kylie's mother. The trip to the bathroom, Amanda seeing that the alarm had been deactivated. As she spoke, she had to forcibly push back the building awareness of the man at her side and the slowly rising hunger. It was like a demon inside her, claws raking at her womb, demanding the hard thrust of his cock, the white-hot release of his semen.

"Rumor drifted in that the hit would be made just after Dash made contact with the Feline Breeds," Stephanie revealed, her voice soft, obviously less antagonistic than the two chest-beaters sharing the vehicle with them. "We were delayed in putting together a plan to protect you when his wife, Elizabeth, went into labor. As soon as they were able to travel, Dash met with your father. He didn't seem to take the threats seriously."

Amanda couldn't control the hitch in her breathing then. Neither her brother nor her father had taken a threat against her seriously? They hadn't even told her?

"You're lying," she whispered then. "My parents wouldn't risk my life."

"They put a damned good detail on you," Kiowa assured her. "The four men protecting you are the best. All he had to go on was a rumor, no hard intelligence. And I believe you refused to move into the White House for any length of time."

Sarcasm colored his voice now.

But he was right, she had refused to move into the official Presidential home for any reason. The fight had been a bitter one. Why hadn't he told her there might have been a threat? She might have changed her mind.

No, she amended that thought, she wouldn't have. She was high on her own independence, her new job, her friends and her home. She would have required proof, not rumor.

"What now?" she asked then.

"Now, we get you to safety then contact your father," Kiowa answered her sharply. "And we keep you there until the vote on Breed Law comes up next week. With your safety assured, President Marion will vote the bill in rather than shoot it down because you have a gun at your head."

"And since you've mated with a Breed, why everything's just going to be peachy now," Simon drawled mockingly. "Ain't we all lucky?"

She would have jerked up if Kiowa's hand hadn't suddenly pressed her back down.

"What the hell is he talking about?" she snarled, flipping around as she held the blanket close to her nakedness.

"Ignore him. He's a twit," Kiowa advised, his voice dangerously soft.

"Funny, he doesn't sound like a twit. An asshole maybe, but not a twit," she pointed out furiously. "Why did he say that?"

"Because he wants to cause trouble. Simon likes causing trouble. Don't you, Simon?"

Amanda did not trust his tone of voice in the least.

"Oh yeah, trouble is just my middle name, ain't it, Steph?" he drawled.

"Or something," she replied. The underlying messages were driving Amanda crazy.

"You're lying to me," she told Kiowa then. "Why lie to me now?"

He breathed in roughly. "Look, Manda, it's about as clear as daylight that you don't want to know anything more than you already do. Just stay down and leave things alone for now. We'll talk later."

"I don't want to talk later," she replied with all the false sweetness she could muster. "I want to talk now. I want to know why the hell he called me your mate and just exactly what being a mate entails."

His brow lifted sardonically. "As you stated earlier, you are very well aware of what an animal is. You figure it out."

She could feel herself paling. It didn't help the heat building in her pussy.

"What did you do to me?" Fury was enveloping her. Unfortunately, it was driving a less wanted heat higher.

His teeth flashed as he smiled. There, at the side of his mouth, his canines glittered savagely. Her shoulder ached as though in response, the heat there spreading through her.

"Do you really want to know, Manda?" he asked, his voice dangerously rough, leaning closer as she stared up at him with wide eyes. "Or would you rather just stay nice and peaceful right now, and let that heat just simmer in your snug little cunt rather than burning out of control? Keep pushing, and baby, it's going to burn."

She remembered the burn. And it was getting there.

"I don't like being treated like a child," she snapped in response. "Stop trying to hide things from me."

"I've treated you like a child?" He growled. "Maybe you don't remember some of the more memorable moments we spent together. Want me to remind you?"

His hand went for the blanket.

"Fuck. Duck and cover. We have choppers coming in low."

Kiowa ducked and jerked the blanket until it covered them both, head to toe, insulating them in the center of a cauldron of heat as the heavy throb of helicopters broke the silence of the night.

"We have Breed soldiers ahead of us and behind us. Enough firepower to take out a militia, and we're close to the compound," he assured her, jerking her closer to his body as he lay half over her.

"Don't." He was pressing against her nakedness now, one hand low at her back, his bare chest rasping her nipples.

She didn't give a damn about choppers. The flames were beating at her brain, burning through her body. Her senses couldn't think of anything else or remember anything else except the feel of him pressing into her, moving in her, swelling...

She whimpered as more of her juices spilled from her pussy, preparing her for him, making the need bloom within her with a force she knew she couldn't deny for long.

What had happened? It still made no sense that her body would overrule her mind and force her surrender to a man that, first, she didn't know, and second, wasn't even her species. But it made little difference to her body as her nipples pressed into his chest, burning with the need for his touch.

"Please don't touch me," she sighed against him. How was she supposed to control the fires whipping through her body when she could feel him so close? The length of his body pressed against hers, the tempting pleasure of his cock pressing against her lower stomach, shielded only by the material of his jeans.

He stared back at her, his expression brooding as her fingers pressed against his shoulders, caressed the hard muscles of his arms. She couldn't stand not touching him. Her body hungered for him, craved him.

His hand moved slowly then, his fingers cupping the curve of her cheek, his thumb smoothing over her lips.

"It's going to happen again, Amanda." He kept his voice low, controlled. "How much longer do you think either of us can deny it?"

The danger had receded into the back of her mind. She didn't care who was following them, what the helicopters were doing, or how close they were to safety. All she cared about was Kiowa pressing close to her, his body warming her.

"Don't get all hot and bothered, boys and girls," Simon snapped. "They're coming in for another pass. They go for three and we're on shoot and run. We're close enough to make it and we have troops on standby."

"This is turning into a fucking fiasco," Kiowa muttered as he stared down at her, his eyes hot and glittering with demand. "Flat in the middle of a likely war zone and all I want to do is fuck you again."

Her eyes fluttered closed. She wanted to be strong. She really did want to be strong. She needed to be strong, to deny the frantic lust beating at her brain.

"I can smell your heat, Manda," he whispered then, causing her eyes to fly open in alarm. "It smells like honey syrup. And I'm really partial to honey."

She trembled convulsively as his hand slid between her thighs, his fingers moving through the glaze of moisture there before he retreated. Shock held her captive as he lifted his hand then, her juices laying thick on his fingers and brought them to his mouth and allowed his tongue to move slowly, erotically over his fingers, licking them clean.

Her breath shuddered from her body as a whimper broke free of her lips.

"Okay, we fucking got problems." The Jeep veered sharply as the sound of gunfire echoed around them.

Amanda watched Kiowa's expression change. Passion receded. It didn't disappear, just receded as cold hard fury tightened his face.

"Stay down."

He pushed her in close to the wheel cover as he moved from beneath the blanket, jerking a lethal black weapon from the floorboard as the back window lowered.

His back rippled with muscles, his lean, corded body tense and ready for action. Her pussy convulsed and the fear of death was nothing compared to the fear of never fucking this man again.

"How many?" he yelled out as Amanda's eyes flew to the window beside her.

"Just the one. We're twenty minutes from the compound. They have a chopper lifting up any second but damn if I want any bullets hitting this vehicle. They took shots at Taber's car behind us. They don't know which vehicle we're in yet."

"They knew where to look for us, though," Kiowa snapped.

"Yeah. This is bad shit," Simon agreed. "Get ready, he's coming in again!"

"Stay all the way down Amanda," Kiowa snapped as she started to lean up. "Down and covered, dammit."

His voice was so hard, so vicious she jerked the blanket over her head and huddled against the side of the vehicle.

"Here comes Kane on a fast pass," Simon yelled out. "Let's see if he can draw them out."

The hard throb of the helicopter and the sound of a speeding vehicle filled her ears. Tight curses and gunfire exploded in the night.

"Fuck this."

The sound of Kiowa's voice had Amanda peeking out. Her heart jumped in her throat as she watched him move his body through the window, bracing his hips against the window frame as he began to return fire.

"Dammit it, Kiowa..." Simon was cursing, Stephanie was joining Kiowa.

Amanda jerked up, eyes wide, her gaze trying to fly in all directions.

Two vehicles were behind them, one at their side and two ahead of them and in seconds there were bodies hanging out of all of them, firing at the helicopter streaking toward them.

White flares of light exploded from the aircraft ahead as gunfire pelted around them while it veered to the side.

"Shit. Shit," Simon was screaming now. "Tanner's coming in with the Breed chopper, kids. This is gonna get ugly."

Another helicopter flew in like a kamikaze on speed. It flew low over the vehicles before tilting and turning to meet the other. Amanda couldn't see a damn thing, no matter where she looked, she could only hear it.

The sound of machine-gun fire and overhead blasts filled the night before an explosion lit the night sky and Kiowa let out a war whoop that would have done an Apache on a late night western proud.

"That boy doesn't have the sense God gave suicide candidates," Simon snarled as the helicopter dipped low and waved side to side. "Do you know the fucking press this is going to get? Callan's going to kick all our damned asses."

Amanda didn't have the change to think or ask questions on any of it as Kiowa swung back into the Jeep, jerked her close and stole her lips in a kiss that stole her mind.

"Fuck!" Simon's voice was the last thing she heard.

Kiowa thrust his tongue deep into her mouth, the swollen extension curling around hers as she closed her lips on it helplessly. Honey and spice. Male heat and demand.

It poured into her as her hands gripped his head, her fingers tangling into his hair as he groaned into her kiss. Adrenaline, lust and fear combined to slam her senses into overdrive and send her soaring.

There was no fear, no concerns when she was feeding from the passion of his kiss. Lips and tongues twisted together, fractured moans echoing within the insulated veil that lust weaved around them. Nothing else existed. Time stopped moving. There was only Kiowa.

Chapter Eleven

ဢ

Kiowa was enraged, horny, and in the mood to kill. Unfortunately the fucking bastards pissing him off didn't have the balls to face him. That left only friendlies to pound on. You couldn't kill a friendly, but you could damned sure knock the hell out of the one that got you in this mess to begin with, he thought, as the Jeep slammed to a stop inside the Feline Breed compound right beside Dash Sinclair.

He slammed the door open, stepped from the vehicle and planted his fist in the other man's face first thing. Fury surged through his body as he ignored the gathering Feline Breeds. Let them try to interfere, he thought as he growled warningly at the lot of them, flashing the curved canines at the side of his mouth. By God, he would lay them out too.

Dash landed on his back, shook his head then speared Kiowa with a long, cold look.

"That one was free," he said quietly as he came to his feet. "Don't make the mistake of taking another."

Kiowa lifted his lip in a feral snarl before he hit him again.

"Goddamn it, Kiowa!" Dash remained on his feet, just barely.

"You dirty fucking bastard," Kiowa growled furiously. "Remind to never, never, take another job you throw my way. I don't need your fucking messes; I make enough of my own. I was doing real damned fine where I was at. What made you even think I needed this bullshit?"

His cock was raging. The smell of Amanda's heat locked in his brain and he couldn't escape it.

"Yeah, you were real content," Dash snorted, watching him warily as the Breeds milled around them. "Fun was it, Kiowa, playing bouncer in a scum pit?"

Kiowa snarled again as Callan stepped closer, almost close enough to scent Amanda's pulsing arousal, to smell that intriguing soft scent of honey and spice.

The other man backed up, an amused grin tilting his lips as amber eyes regarded him with no hint of wariness. Fucking cats, he thought furiously.

"Look, Kiowa, we have a cabin ready for you and all the explanations you need." Dash was obviously fighting his amusement despite his sore face. "Get back in the jeep and we'll drive up there and talk all you want."

"Do you think I'm in the mood to fucking talk?" Kiowa snarled. "Point out the goddamned cabin then get the fuck out of my way."

The erection in his pants was killing him, and Amanda's low moan from the back of the Jeep was like a spike of lust slamming into his guts.

Dash's eyes narrowed again. "Shit. You kissed her again, didn't you? Dammit, that only makes it worse," he muttered. "Kiowa, haven't you figured it out yet?"

"Point the cabin out, you mangy fucking wolf," Kiowa growled, the unbidden, guttural sound of his own voice was shocking. "Then get the hell out of my way."

Dash sighed in frustration. "Up the hill. Second cabin under the tree line."

Kiowa glanced up the graveled road that headed into the mountain before turning and stalking to the Jeep.

"Get out of my way," he muttered when Simon didn't move from his position in front of the door of the driver's side.

Simon laughed, a low, mocking chuckle as he slid smoothly to the side.

"Have fun, coyote boy." The smile on his face had Kiowa growling again. Dammit, what the hell was he doing mixed up in this crazy mess? he thought.

A second later, the Jeep spun from its parking place and headed up the short distance to the cabin Dash had pointed out. Blood pounded hard and fast in his veins as Amanda rose behind him, her arms curling around his neck as her lips moved over the pulse throbbing hard and hot at the side of his neck.

She licked the pulsing vein slowly, then her sharp little teeth bit down on the tough skin as the Jeep skidded to the side of the road before Kiowa managed to right it, punch the gas and curse.

"You bit me," she sighed at his ear.

"I'm going to bite you again." His teeth ached to bite her again. To feel the soft flesh that bordered neck and shoulder beneath the sharp canines as he held her to him, his cock swelling…knotting her… He groaned at the thought and brought the Jeep to a shuddering stop at the door of the cabin.

He didn't bother with the blanket that wrapped around her when he jerked the back door open. He just grabbed her, pressed her to the side of the Jeep and tore frantically at his jeans.

He wasn't going to make it into the little house. He didn't have the strength to get any further than the feel of her in his arms. Naked except for the red stockings and stiletto ankle boots, her legs curving around his waist, the naked heat of her pussy burning the head of his dick.

He lifted her, his hands gripping her ass, tugging the soft swell of flesh apart as he poised at the entrance of her cunt.

"Scream for me," he whispered then. "I want to hear your cries."

His body tightened as her breath caught, her eyes gleaming in the predawn light as he began to work the head of his cock into the tight, God so fucking tight, pussy weeping its siren's call.

Her head fell back against the jeep, long silken strands of hair flowing around her as the first, throttled cry left her throat.

* * * * *

Amanda gripped Kiowa's hips tighter with her knees, her gaze meeting his as she felt the hard spurt of fluid enter her before his cock did. Whatever it was, it alternately burned and eased her. She could feel her muscles relaxing even as her arousal reached new peaks.

She couldn't deny him. It was beyond her strength, beyond her ability to turn away from the pleasure of his touch. Whatever was wrong with her, whatever had been done to her, for this moment in time, she was more animal than woman in this hunger for the man touching her.

With each hard pulse of the fluid, his cock slid deeper inside her, stretching her, the pleasure building as fiery lashes of sensation shredded reality around her.

She screamed, just as he wanted her to, because the fine line between pleasure and pain was so exquisite.

"Kiowa." Tears came to her eyes as she felt him fill her, sliding so deep and hot inside her pussy that she knew she could never forget the feel of him. It would be with her forever. And that terrified her.

"God, Manda, I'm sorry." He was panting as he worked his erection deeper, his hands clenching in the smooth muscles of her buttocks, spreading them erotically.

She could feel the little pinch of fire in her anal opening as he did that. The gentle pull of her flesh parting her just enough to make her anus flex in response. There were too many sensations whipping through her mind, too much to process at once as he finally lodged to the hilt inside her convulsing pussy.

Her hands dug into his shoulders as she screamed out her pleasure then, white-hot liquid fire rushing through her loins and sending her spinning on a lust-filled voyage. She was stretched to her limits, his cock burning her, throbbing inside her like another heartbeat as his teeth scrapped her lower neck.

He was going to bite her again. The little scrape of his teeth against the wound already there didn't hurt as it should. When his tongue licked over it, she shuddered with a pleasure she couldn't have expected.

"You're so tight." His words caused her to flex around his cock, tighten on him in pleasure even as fire struck her nerves from the movement.

His hips flexed as he drew back, pulling out until only the head remained before surging inside her again.

It was so good. It was too good.

She gasped, fighting for breath as he caressed her with the thick width of his erection, stroking nerves she never knew existed. Her head tossed against the window of the Jeep as he began a hard pounding rhythm inside her then. There were few preliminaries, but she didn't need any. Her juices were flowing thick and hot around him, aided by the occasional hot pulses of pre-semen from his cock.

She didn't know men did that. Or maybe they didn't.

She whimpered as she remembered who and what was fucking her so thoroughly.

And he was fucking her thoroughly. Her thighs tightened further as she fought to move with him, the controlled strokes hammering inside her kept her on the edge, held her back from the fall.

"Don't you come yet, dammit," he growled at her ear as she arched and writhed on the thick cock penetrating her, impaling her. "Not yet, Manda. Not yet."

"Yes!" She screamed her objection, bracing her knees against him and trying to ride him harder.

His hands tightened on her ass for a second. Then one released her.

A second later he backed from the Jeep, turning and bracing his own back against it as his hand landed against her ass. The burning little sting had her gasping, her pussy rippling in nearing orgasm.

"Not yet," he snarled then.

"Now." She was shaking, the added little pain pushing her higher.

He spanked her again. His hard calloused hand landed with enough strength to make her burn. She twisted, tightening her pussy, feeling her juices flowing with added stimulus.

"Damn you," he gritted out then. "You're killing me, Manda. Leave me some control, dammit."

Why? She had none left.

She tightened again, whimpering in pleasure as his strokes increased, his hands gripping her ass as he began to pound inside her. Hard. Heavy.

Burning, exquisite lightning erupted inside her womb, sending her senses spinning as ecstasy washed over with an orgasm so deep, so hard she could only cry brokenly in response.

Then she screamed.

"No. Kiowa, no..."

But there was no stopping it. The swelling had already begun, stretching her, prolonging her orgasm, locking him deep inside her as his hips jerked and his throttled shout signaled his own release.

His semen spurted inside her, and she could feel it. Felt the head of his cock locked at the mouth of her womb as each hard pulse of seed jetted inside her body. Her release built again, exploded, echoed and vibrated inside her as his teeth sank into her flesh again, holding her in place, refusing to allow her to fight the hold he now had on her.

Tears washed from her eyes as he held her close. Pleasure was a steady, vibrating force inside her body, rocking her over and over again even as fear filled her mind. What he was doing to her wasn't normal. It wasn't human.

Had she asked for this? she wondered distantly. Had her lustful imaginings, her need for that flare of pain with her pleasure brought her to this?

"Manda." His teeth lifted from her shoulder.

Why didn't it hurt? she wondered. When his canines pierced her flesh, why wasn't there a horrible pain instead of that blinding, mind-consuming pleasure?

"Don't cry, baby."

He was still locked inside her, trembling every few seconds as another pulse of seed filled her womb.

"It's going to be okay."

Was it? How could it be?

Her tears wet his perspiration-damp flesh further as she shuddered in his arms. She could feel it. The swelling inside her was large enough to keep her pussy flexing, to keep the echoes of her release washing through her. It was tight enough that no matter how she fought, how she shifted, it didn't budge. It held his cock in place, kept him anchored to her as the final hot blasts of semen filled her.

She felt the change then. Slowly, the swelling eased, too slowly.

Amanda whimpered as she fought to calculate her cycles and ovulation and realized the time for this was much too close. She couldn't allow this to continue. She couldn't become a slave to whatever effect he had on her.

She fought for composure as he finally pulled free of her, fighting and failing to hold back her moan at the pleasure of that last stroke.

He didn't release her though. He shifted her in his arms then carried her into the little cabin. He didn't speak and neither did she. What was there to say?

She was fucking a stranger, a man she didn't know and had never seen before last night. A man that was an animal.

The Breed controversy had not touched her. Not during her father's campaign or his election. Breed Law was something she hadn't considered too closely for that same fact. It hadn't touched her. But now it was. Touching her so intimately, in such ways that she wondered if she would survive it.

Chapter Twelve

$\wp$

"Get a bath. I'll call down to the main house and see about clothes." He sat her in the middle of the surprisingly large bathroom, beside a deep Jacuzzi tub that she knew her sore muscles were going to fall in love with.

The rough log walls were thick, well sanded and painted a dark redwood. White filling bisected each log and made for an attractive contrast. The tub sat on the far wall with a white porcelain sink a few feet from it. Over a bit more was the toilet; the opposite wall, a wardrobe that Kiowa pulled several towels and a washrag from. He sat a bag of Epsom salts on the sink beside her.

"I'll get something fixed to eat," he continued. "Then we can rest for a while before you have to face anything more."

His expression was closed. Not cold, just unemotional. She had never realized the difference before now. Her father and brother had a habit of going stone-cold when angry or during political confrontations. You could feel the ice coming off them. But not Kiowa. He was just unemotional. Not hot, not cold, as though he just really didn't give a fuck.

Amanda sat down on the small stool at the side of the tub and began unlacing her boots. She kicked them from her feet, then glanced up as she realized he hadn't left.

"I'm not an animal." His voice hadn't changed, neither had his expression. He made a statement, nothing more.

She had called him an animal. She glanced away, fighting back the anxiety growing in her chest as he continued to watch her.

"I don't want this," she said then, staring at the dark wood floor, the colorful rug laid out in front of the tub. "I didn't ask you to do this to me."

Even now the heat hadn't faded from her body. She could have taken him again, easily. Her skin was sensitive, her nipples engorged and dark red rather than the soft pink they had been days before. Her breasts were tight, still swollen and she ached for the taste of his kiss. Her mouth watered for it.

"You don't always get to ask for what life throws at you," he said then. Unemotional. God she hated that. Only then she realized how much more comforting her father and brother's chilling politeness could be. At least she knew it indicated some feeling. There was no feeling here.

She moved to the elastic at the top of her stockings. They were torn in several places, the red silk ruined. She didn't bother taking them off with any care, just stripped them from her legs as she ignored his quiet statement.

"I'll call for some clothes." He could have been talking about the weather as he turned his back on her. "Take your time."

Take your time. As though she had plenty of it.

Was her father worried? Surely he was; he would have been notified the minute her security detail in the apartment next to her didn't check in. As much as she hated the thought of them before, she was comforted by it now. At least he would know she was in trouble.

He and her brother Alexander would come for her. If they could find her.

She shivered at the thought before flipping on the water, adjusting the temperature to as hot as she could stand it, and watching the tub fill up slowly.

It was surreal, this situation. The day before she had nothing bigger on her mind than class subjects and hoping the kids weren't too hyped on chocolate when they returned to school Monday.

Breed Law hadn't been a major concern for her. Her father's Presidency was something she just wanted to ignore. She had been independent, free and enjoying it. Now what was she?

She pushed her fingers ruthlessly through her hair. If she wasn't pregnant yet then she would likely soon be. The timing was too close and the angle and position of his cock as he locked inside her didn't give her much hope that some of his little buddies wouldn't hit home base.

She shuddered at the thought. Oh God, what the hell had she managed to get herself mixed up in? And why would a Wolf Breed, a breed almost unheard of, be close enough to her home to help her?

She knew there was much more going on here than her mind had been able to assimilate in the past hours. Following conversations hadn't exactly penetrated the haze of lust that overwhelmed her. That was trying to overwhelm her now.

She shook her head before stepping in the tub and turning the pulsing jets on full blast. Maybe she should have tried a cold bath.

Kiowa stood silently in the doorway of the kitchen, staring at the men lounging lazily in the living room.

Dash Sinclair and Simon straddled two of the kitchen chairs that had been placed in front of the fireplace. Kane Tyler sat back, too relaxed, in the comfortable recliner set on the left. To the right, Callan and Taber sat on the couch, watching him closely.

They hadn't said much since entering moments before. Kiowa had taken the gown and change of clothes they had brought to the bedroom and laid them on the bed, letting Amanda know they were there.

Now, he stood uncomfortably before the five men watching him, his cock all too aware of the woman still soaking in the bathtub in the other room.

84

"I don't have all night here," he finally informed them, pushing back his anger over the situation and his concerns. "What the fuck is going on?"

Dash sighed, shaking his head as Simon snickered.

"Boy, it's going to be fun watching these hard heads until news hits about this," Simon chuckled. "You guys can get so comical when you're all confused."

"Shut up, Simon," Dash kept his voice quiet, though it vibrated with amusement.

Kiowa stared at each man in turn.

"I'm not in the best fucking mood." His smile was all teeth. He made certain of it. "As a matter of fact, I could kill real easy right now. Answers, gentlemen."

Dash leaned forward, linking his hands in front of him, his brows lowering.

"You mated her," he said simply. "The Breeds have a unique biological reaction to their mates. Your tongue swells, small glands at the side becoming enlarged. Those glands release a hormone, a very potent aphrodisiac that binds you with the woman until either a. she becomes pregnant, or b. ovulation passes and she hasn't conceived. The process can begin at anytime, and continues until either one or the other occurs. After ovulation passes with no pregnancy, it will ease after the initial intensity, but it never goes away. She's yours. Period."

Kiowa stayed completely still. He didn't so much as bat an eyelash or draw in a deeper breath.

"No cure for it?" he asked.

"None," Dash answered. "It's stronger in some, lesser in others. From what I've seen, your mating with Ms. Marion is one of the most intense."

"What if I ignore it?" Oh yeah, he thought, he could do that. When hell froze over.

"Not possible," Callan said. "At least not to this point. The hunger in the female becomes so painful it's intolerable. At least in our experience. I believe it was less so in Dash's case from what little he's told us."

Kiowa stared back at the men, the information flashing through his brain as he fought to find solutions now.

"Have any tests been run on the women?" he asked.

"Not possible." Callan shook his head. "We've tried, but the reaction and mating is so fierce during the period that actual testing could help, that the females can't bear the touch of another male. Taber and I became more animal than man if anyone attempted to touch them. The male instinct to protect and mate is too strong at that time. And the pain they endure is too intense, even drugs don't help. The hormones overwhelm the drugs and impose their natural coding on the female despite all efforts to reduce it. At this time, there's no way to change that."

"And your female is ovulating, Kiowa," Dash informed him. "I could smell it when you first opened the door to the jeep. She's in full heat."

Fuck. Fuck. Double damned fuck. Kiowa wanted to hit something. Hell, he wanted to kill the bastards who put him in this situation. His gaze slashed to Dash. He could kill him, but goddammit, he actually liked the son of a bitch.

"There are, to count, three mated Feline pairs as well as Dash and Elizabeth as the first recorded Wolf mating," Callan informed him. "If it brings you any comfort, we've found nature to be very generous in her pairings. We love our wives, Kiowa, and they would have been women we would have chosen even without the mating heat."

Fine, well and good, Kiowa thought mockingly. So, because his dick got hard for her while he watched her, and he admitted, harder than normal, then nature thought she could just pull a fast one on him? Just his luck.

"Remind me to refuse you next time you need help," he told Dash politely. "As I said, I was doing fine on my own."

Dash snorted. "Come on, Kiowa, that was a lousy job and you know it."

"Someone has to do the shit work." Kiowa shrugged, though he silently admitted that working as a bouncer wasn't his all-time favorite sport. It was just too damned easy to start with. Scum wasn't that hard to keep track of.

"We have another problem here." Kane leaned forward at that point. "President Marion, at this moment, is willing to trust us with his daughter. I talked to him within seconds after your arrival. Official word will be that she is ill and recuperating in an undisclosed location while his son launches an investigation into the situation. The fact that he's willing to trust us with his daughter indicates his security in Breed honor. He wants to talk to her later, but otherwise agrees it would be foolhardy to head out here and bring more trouble down on her.

"Official report on the helicopter attack was that Callan was attacked while on his way home from meetings in Washington, where he had been earlier. We can keep her safe here until the vote on Breed Law. Then, he'll want to see her."

That gave him a week, Kiowa thought. Not nearly enough time.

"That chopper wasn't government issue either," Taber said. "It was private, and modified for weapons. Communications we intercepted indicates they weren't certain who was in the vehicles though. They were taking a shot and hoping. But if they got other Breeds that was fine too. Innocents didn't matter."

"A week isn't long," Dash said then. "Marion will be here the moment voting is over to see his daughter. We'll have to have answers for him then."

"And that concerns me how?" Kiowa lifted his brow fractionally. "She won't be leaving with him, so he can come now for all I care."

He wasn't certain where that declaration came from, but once it passed his lips he guessed he committed to it.

"There's a ban on relating the information on mating and the mating heat, Kiowa," Callan said then, his voice hard. "If we're to protect ourselves, we need to keep this information hidden from the general population as long as possible. We can't tell Marion why his daughter can't leave. You'll have to convince her to stay."

Kiowa stared back at the Pack Leader for long moments. They were idiots, he thought. What the hell made any of them think that Ms. Amanda Marion was going to agree to anything so outlandish?

"I can gag her." Actually, it wasn't a bad idea.

"Come on, Kiowa," Dash snapped then. "Let's be serious for a few minutes here."

"Fine, then say something serious," he shrugged loosely, careful to keep his body relaxed, to hide the internal fury pouring through him.

His mate thought he was an animal and the swelling inside her sickened her. She had been kidnapped, fucked, and mated and Kiowa didn't see a chance in hell of her accepting any of it easily.

"She's a reasonable woman…" Dash began.

"She's a child." Kiowa crossed his arms over his chest as he stared back at the other man. "She's twenty-four years old, first year out of Daddy's care, and not exactly mature enough to handle the fact that within days she's going to be carrying an animal's ba—" He broke off as he caught sight of movement at the bedroom door.

There she stood, stock-still, the flannel gown Callan had brought her dwarfing her figure, the dark blue color emphasizing the pasty white complexion of her skin. Her scent filled the room then, drawing all eyes to her. Honey and spice, so sweet she made his mouth water as her arousal reach out to him.

He stayed in place, forcing back the impulse to rush to her, to protect her. Dammit, he had enough trouble protecting himself at this point.

She swallowed tightly, her throat working convulsively as she obviously fought to keep her stomach from heaving.

"You talk to her," Kiowa suggested then. "Maybe you can convince her it's really not so bad. What do you think, Amanda? Can you handle carrying my pup?"

She swayed, her hand gripping the doorframe as she went impossibly whiter.

"Fuck, Kiowa," Callan snarled as he jumped to her as her knees buckled while Kiowa forced back the screaming objection as the other man kept her from falling to the floor.

He hadn't believed them, he admitted a second later. When they said she could bear no other male's touch, he hadn't believed them.

Her pain-filled cry shattered his soul the moment Callan touched her, hard shudders racing over her body as she tightened to breaking point, going to her knees from the pain. Kiowa raced across the room, jerking her to him, his arms enfolding her as her hands gripped his waist, dry heaves spasming her body as she fought back the reactive sickness to the Feline's touch.

"Shit," he sighed wearily, one hand cupping her head and holding her close to his chest as she fought for her composure.

"Kiowa, you're a bastard!" Simon snapped furiously.

"Get out of here," Kiowa growled. "Just get the hell out until I can figure out what the hell to do."

He was aware of their gazes locked on him—Callan and Simon's filled with anger, Dash's just quiet, regretful. The emotions filled the air, assaulting his sensitive sense of smell as well as his patience.

"Good luck, buddy," Dash murmured on his way past him. "Good luck."

His hand smoothed down Amanda's hair as she slowly composed herself, the arm around her waist tightening as she pressed herself closer to him. It had to be unconscious, he thought, she wouldn't want his warmth, wouldn't need it. It was biological. An urge brought on by the hormone and the situation nothing more.

She thought he was an animal. And he guessed he was, because it would be a cold day in hell before he would let her go now, no matter what she wanted.

Chapter Thirteen

એ

He thought she was just a child, too immature understand the facts the life.

Amanda moved slowly away from Kiowa after the initial reaction to the other man's touch. The pain had been...horrendous. Every nerve in her body has screamed in agony, rejecting the touch, no matter how helpful.

Moving through the living room, she rubbed her arms slowly, concentrating on just breathing, on allowing the information she had heard to process in her head. She wasn't a stupid person, and she wasn't a child. She had managed to understand every word of what she had overhead. And she had overheard a lot. Too much.

"I didn't mean to call you an animal after..." She waved her hand as she turned back to face him. "I was shocked."

"Yes, you did." He shrugged his broad shoulders as he refused to accept the apology. "I've watched you for a while, Ms. Marion. Several weeks in fact. My impression of you is that you pretty much say what you mean."

"So watching me allows you to form a basis for your opinions?" she asked him curiously, trying to still her anger at his arrogance.

"In most cases." He nodded sharply before moving past her to the kitchen. "I'll fix breakfast then you can sleep. We'll be here for a while, so I guess we'll be bombarded by Callan and Taber's wives as well as their sisters. Damned welcoming party, I guess."

She turned as he entered the kitchen. The half wall between the two rooms allowed her a clear view to what he was doing. Moving about bare-chested, muscles rippling as he moved ingredients out of the refrigerator and onto the counter.

She couldn't exactly call him handsome, though he was definitely unique. At least six feet two inches tall, leanly muscled. If there was an ounce of fat on that body she hadn't found it. And her hands had been in places they shouldn't be.

His thick, devil's black hair fell to his shoulders and when he turned toward her, the stark, well-defined features of his face held her gaze. He was simply mesmerizing. Not handsome, she assured herself. But his sharp nose and well-arched brows over deep black eyes were definitely worth looking at. And his lips.

She really didn't want to look at his lips. But she did. They made her mouth water at the thought of the pleasure to be had there.

"I heard what they said," she said. "About the mating."

He didn't pause, his expression never changed.

"So I assumed," he finally said as he flicked a glance toward her.

"It won't work," she told him. "We can't let this happen, you know we can't."

She couldn't imagine being tied to this man in such a way. If she thought her brother was hard, then Kiowa was pure steel.

"If you can stand it, then so can I." His voice didn't raise; it didn't lower. She had seen him furious, heard him enraged, filled with lust and just plain mocking in the few hours she had been with him. This confused her.

"Kiowa..." She licked her lips nervously. "I don't even know your last name."

"I don't have one." He turned away from her, bent at the waist and dragged a teflon skillet from under the cabinet.

"Everyone has a last name," she said, shaking her head in disbelief. "You have to have one for a social security number, to get a job."

"Innocence is so refreshing," he said. And dammit, his voice didn't change. Unemotional. Flat. She was beginning to appreciate her brother more and more.

"What do you mean by that?" She crossed her arms over her breasts, mostly to hide her hard nipples. He kept looking at them. Though she admitted they were hard to miss.

"I mean, Ms. Marion, that if you move in the right circles, or should I say the wrong circles, you can get away with damned near anything. I have a dozen false identities, social security numbers and passports. All with very illegitimate last names. But I do not have a last name. My mother's family refused to allow me hers, and it's hard for a Breed to claim a father. Therefore, I am, lastnameless."

"School... Birth records..." She shook her head. This was impossible.

"Schooled myself for the most part." He filled the skillet with bacon. Evidently he ate a lot. "My grandfather kept me hidden in the mountains after I was weaned from my mother. As I grew older, he left me there alone. He always provided books, though. Television. I wasn't deprived."

She blinked in shock. "That's not a childhood," she whispered.

"I wasn't a child." He looked at her again, his eyes dull. "I was an animal, Ms. Marion. One he had no choice but to protect because his honor demanded it. His blood was in my veins whether he liked it or not. He did his best."

There was acceptance in his voice. No regret, no recriminations, no anger or pain. Just acceptance.

"You're not an animal," she snapped, trembling in shock that anyone would treat a child so cruelly. "I said I was sorry. I was..." She drew in a hard, deep breath. "I was frightened, Kiowa. I reacted and it was wrong."

He stared at her for a long moment before turning away, dismissing her as though she didn't matter. God, this was hard. The lust rising in her body wasn't making it any easier.

"Tell me," he said then, turning back to her as the bacon sizzled on the stove. "What will you do when you're swelling with my child, knowing you had no choice in its conception, that you've whelped a child that is as much an animal as it is human? Will you hold it to your breast and cuddle it with love? Or will you give it to strangers to raise? Will you give that child your name? Or will you attempt to kill it before it has a chance to draw its first breath?"

He worked quickly to open canned biscuits and lay them in a baking pan as Amanda stared back at him miserably.

"I wouldn't choose abortion," she whispered.

He looked up at her again as he slid the pan in the oven.

"Will you give me my child?"

There. Emotion. She saw for just a second, bleak, pain-ridden. A glimmer of fury in his eyes before he shut it away.

"No," she said then, knowing that any child she carried would have her heart.

He braced his hands on the counter and nodded slowly, his gaze turned to the floor for long seconds. When he looked back up at her, the possessive glitter that filled his eyes caused her to take a careful step back.

"If you heard much at all, then you know the full truth," he said tightly. "You're my mate, bound to me whether either of us likes it or not. I won't let you go."

She shook her head slowly.

"You will," she whispered softly. "Because you won't want a woman that was forced upon you, Kiowa. One that doesn't share your dreams, your needs, or the future you want to pursue. I don't want your future," she said painfully. "I have my own dreams."

"And your child that you refuse to give up?" he snapped. "What part will it play?"

"My child will be just that. Mine. I would love it, give it my name. I would treasure it."

"But not his father?" Those eyes were alive now, and fury fed them.

"What do you want me to say?" she cried desperately. "You're trying to hurt me, to wrap me in guilt and make me feel responsible for this. I'm not."

"That's a child's response," he bit out. "An adult adapts, Amanda. You're right; when this is over you're most likely better off leaving. A child could never handle me, let alone my life or the difficulties involved in raising my kid. My kid, lady. I'll be damned if my kid will be treated like an animal by anyone. Nor will it be raised without its father."

She fought to control her breathing, the racing of her blood. She could feel the arousal building with it and she couldn't afford the weakness. Not now.

"You're being unreasonable," she argued. "I don't even know you. And to be perfectly honest, I don't think I like you much. What basis is that for raising children?"

"A hell of a lot better than I had." He flipped the bacon with a furious motion of the spatula.

What could she say to that?

"Wolf Breeds will be accepted after the Breed Law enacts…"

A hard, mocking laugh left his throat then as he speared her with those black eyes of his.

"Wolf breeds?" he asked her softly. "What does that have to do with me, Amanda?"

She licked her lips nervously.

"That's what you are…" He was shaking his head before she finished.

"No, baby," he said silkily. "It wasn't a Wolf breed that knotted in that tight pussy of yours. It was one of those nasty old Coyote Breeds. How acceptable is that?"

Chapter Fourteen

ဢ

"*Coyote Breeds are considered the vermin of the Breeds,*" her father told Alexander thoughtfully as they went over the Breed Law Act that the Feline Breeds had submitted. "*They are said to be soulless. Without redemption. They were created to be the jailors, lapdogs to the scientists and military personnel that oversaw the other Breeds.*"

"*Is there anyway to adapt the law to exclude them?*" her brother asked, his pale gray eyes resting thoughtfully on the papers spread out on the table in her father's private living room.

"*We can't exclude them without raising more questions,*" her father shook his head slowly. "*The Feline Pride leader has suggested allowing them to handle the situation on an individual basis. They'll police the different Breeds as needed.*"

"*It's going to be hard to do...*" Alexander murmured.

"*Aren't they human as well, Vernon?*" her mother asked gently. "*Humanity can overcome a lot of things, even selective breeding. You're talking about men here, not animals.*"

Her mother, Delaney Marion had a voice like silk and a heart as soft as a marshmallow. But she made sense. As Amanda listened to the conversation and studied for the all-important final test before receiving her teaching certificate, she admitted her mother's argument made more sense than any others she had heard.

"*In this case, we'll have no choice but to pray that's true,*" her father sighed, running his fingers through his thick, gray hair. "*But the Coyote Breeds are going to be trouble, Della, you can bet on it. I can feel it.*" Her father's instincts were always good.

"*They're animals,*" her brother had stated, his voice icy cold, his eyes matching the tone as he looked up. "*They'll be more than trouble, they'll be a blight. We should just give Lyons sanction to kill them all like the diseased creatures they are."*

The memory wasn't a pleasant one. As Amanda ate the breakfast Kiowa fixed and fought the lust rising within her, the memory taunted her. So far, the Feline Breeds were being accepted reasonably well by the world. The reports of their creation, treatment by their creators and the plans to use them against the general population were horrifying. The fact that so many Breeds had died rather than kill, and fought so hard for their freedom redeemed them in society's eyes. Reports of the Coyote were another story. They were created and trained to guard and hunt the others. The reports on that Breed were terrifying. Vicious, bloodthirsty, as cruel as their handlers.

But Kiowa was none of those. He was a man, with plenty of faults, she admitted, but he wasn't bloodthirsty. If he had been, he would have helped the kidnappers rather than rescuing her. The Feline Breed leader seemed to accept him well enough; he actually seemed to like him from what Amanda had seen.

"Stop thinking so hard." Kiowa moved her empty plate from in front of her as well as the glass that had held the milk he forced on her.

She watched him curiously as he washed up quickly.

"I need to take a shower." He placed the last dish in the drainer minutes later. "Stay in the cabin. The mountains are heavily patrolled by Feline guards and they don't know you yet. We also have several trained wolves and a mountain lion or two patrolling. They definitely won't like you. If you don't smell like a cat, they eat you."

She knew her expression reflected her shock.

"Go on to bed and try to sleep. It's been a hell of a night."

Weariness seemed to drag at her anyway, but it did little to dim the need burning bright in her womb.

"Where are you sleeping?" she asked him.

He stiffened.

"On the couch. If you need me, just let me know. I won't bother you otherwise."

If she could handle it. The words seemed to linger in the air around them despite the fact that she hadn't voiced them.

Could she handle it?

Could she handle the consequences if she didn't?

"How did your mother conceive you?" She didn't know where the question came from.

He watched her closely for several, long moments.

"She was taken while coming home from college one night. The Breed scientists often kidnapped their breeders. If they were ovulating, they kept them and bred them. If they weren't, they tried to force ovulation. If they couldn't make them take, then they let them go."

"How did your mother escape?"

"She was ovulating. She was artificially inseminated with the altered sperm and then locked in a cage. A week later, tests were negative for conception. They released her. Evidently, there are very few women compatible enough with the altered genetics to actually allow conception."

"How was it negative?"

He smiled sarcastically. "You're a smart one aren't you? Coyote sperm is evidently viable for much longer periods of time within the female womb. Up to two weeks was the latest report I believe. The unique hormone created by the altered genetics can also force ovulation on its own. As it did with my mother, I guess.

"Once they learned this, they started searching for the breeders they had turned loose. It was years later unfortunately. Shit happens. My mother died in a car crash when I was five, no one but my grandfather knew of my existence. Even her new husband had no idea I existed. By then, there was no checking the body for previous birth since she was more or less cremated in the crash. Too bad, so sad. Kiowa got away."

"Then…" Her heart was racing in her chest now, a hard anxious beat that unfortunately had negative results.

"You're ovulating now." He nodded. "I've locked inside you twice and chances are you have all kinds of little Coyote sperm racing around in your womb. But you might hit it lucky, baby. As I said, most Breed sperm isn't compatible with a normal female. Chances are good it won't catch."

That was not regret she heard in his voice, she reassured herself.

"I'll go to bed." She rose quickly to her feet and headed out of the room.

She had to think, but thinking and being in the same room with Kiowa wasn't going to work.

Immature, he had called her. A child. Unfortunately she wanted to rage at him just as she would have her father or brother when they were doing something unreasonable or enforcing a rule she disagreed with. If it were merely a question of disagreeing, then she would be in his face now.

From what she had overheard, it was much more than that. The hormone that was making her crazy for his touch was no more his fault then it was hers, though. How could she fight that?

"You do that." His quiet snarl behind her pricked at her heart and she didn't even know why.

Chapter Fifteen

ઠ

How was she supposed to sleep? Her mind wouldn't settle, but even worse, neither would her body. She stared at the dimly lit ceiling, tracking the fragile motes of light that managed to slip through the heavy dark curtains and tried to find some way to accept this new reality she had been dragged into.

Kiowa was furious. She could see that now. Where her father and brother turned icy, letting their anger freeze rather than burn, Kiowa pushed it back. He buried it under years of acceptance, beneath the tragedy of a childhood that never was and dreams he didn't dare have.

She remembered the look on his face when he pulled from her, his swollen cock popping free of her, the knot barely subsided as she stared up at him in horror that first time.

An animal she had called him.

His expression had shut down immediately, becoming quiet, emotionless, as he calmly left the Jeep. It had been the anger. He fought it, just as she fought for freedom. Now, his anger was escaping and she was bound to one person in a way she feared she would never truly be free of.

If what she had overheard Callan saying was true, then nature had taken her choice away from her.

She turned to her side, curling into a tight ball and pushed back the need lancing through her body. It was getting worse. Horribly worse. She closed her eyes and tried counting sheep, she bit her lip until she tasted blood. She covered her head with the blankets, but the ache just grew and grew.

Her breasts were so tight and swollen she feared her nipples would burst. The touch of her own hands against them sent sensation ripping to her womb, warning her she was in for a long hard battle if she meant to deny what her body hungered for.

Would she have wanted him even without the hormone building in her system? She would have, she thought, remembering his natural inclination to touch her as she had always dreamed of being touched. His teeth tormenting her nipples. His hand landing hard and heavy on the waxed mound of her pussy.

She flinched at the thought as a white-hot streak of remembered pleasure seared that swollen button of nerves. And his cock. She clenched her thighs at the thought of it. The pleasure pain of being impaled on that thick stalk had her juices flowing thick and heavy from her hungry cunt.

She moaned in bleak of acceptance of the fact that she would only be able to fight the arousal for so long. The building pain was almost an agony, her womb clenching, spasming as the withdrawal tore through her.

Withdrawal. That was exactly what it felt like. Her body was protesting the absence of Kiowa's, demanding his touch, demanding the heat and strength that was so much a part of him.

Amanda couldn't believe anything could hurt so bad. That arousal could become agony, tearing at the nerve endings and burning into the mind. She had to get away from him. Maybe if she could just get entirely away from him, then it would stop. Withdrawal needed a source, take the source and the body would adjust. Wouldn't it? It would go back to normal, she could go back to normal. She just had to get away from Kiowa.

Some distant part of her mind was aware that she wasn't thinking rationally. That the building pain and the need for his touch were becoming so extreme that her ability to process reality wasn't as it should be.

She stumbled from the bed, throwing the blankets aside as her feet tangled in them and weaved her way desperately for the living room. Silence filled the cabin, and rather distantly, she remembered a door closing just after Kiowa left the shower.

Had he left her alone? Didn't the heat affect him as it did her?

The bastard, of course it wouldn't.

"Amanda?" He moved from another room instead, one she hadn't paid any attention to on the other side of the living room.

He wore his jeans low, several metal buttons undone. His cock was thick and hard beneath the material.

"Kiowa." She clenched her fists as his scent wrapped around her, drugging her with the need to taste him.

"You should be sleeping." His voice was soft, regretful as he watched her.

He didn't move from the doorway, just stood there, his dark eyes bleak and filled with hunger and need.

"Do you hurt too?" she whispered, feeling her juices trickle down the inside of her thigh.

"Yeah, baby, I hurt too," he said, his voice rough, a low growl of hunger that had her breath catching in her chest.

"It hurts too badly." She shuddered with the pain.

"You know the alternative, Manda." His tone hardened. He wasn't going to let her hide; he wasn't going to let her forget.

"I would love my child," she cried out desperately. "I would."

She would never force it to be alone, to hunger for love or attention. She would lavish praise on it, laugh with it, love it.

"And what of its father, Manda?" he asked her.

Tears fell from her eyes as her head tilted back and a low, painful moan filled the room.

"I don't want to love you," she whispered. "I don't even know you. How can I love you?"

"Yes, you do." He was closer now. "You know me better than you think you do. You know I'll protect you, Manda. You know I'll hold you close and keep you warm. You know you are my mate. Mates are forever. Just as you know your body will never go hungry for mine, your every desire, your every need fulfilled."

Her head titled forward, something inside her shattering at his words. Sexuality was something to hide where she came from. God help her if her family every found her books, or discovered her perversions. But Kiowa knew them. He knew what she wanted, what her body craved. Marriages survived on less than that; surely a mating wouldn't be too bad?

Your hormones are talking, her mind screamed out. *Buck up girl. Remember, freedom? Time to be alone?*

Time to be alone with her books and her daydreams, she thought. Kiowa was a sexual fantasy come to life.

"You're manipulating me." She was panting for air.

"Of course I am." He shrugged carelessly. "You weren't far off the mark when you called me an animal, baby. Those instincts are alive and humming and they're screaming you're mine. I won't let you go, Amanda."

"God you are such a headache," she snapped, perspiration covering her body as lust built to a fever-pitch. "Do you have any idea how impossible this is? This isn't my life. It isn't what I want."

"This wasn't your life." He leaned lazily against the doorframe then. "It is now. You take the scraps life throws at you and make the best of it. You're a smart woman, smart enough to know this isn't something that's just going to go away."

"That doesn't mean I have to just bow down and give in to it," she argued fiercely. "Scientists created this curse you have, they can fix it."

He laughed at that.

"Do you think your eggheaded God-complex scientists had any clue what they were doing?" he asked mockingly. "Do you have any idea the strong, vital men and women who died, created to be killers, but born with such honor and intelligence that their creators knew they could never let them live? No, Amanda, the world's best and brightest are currently living in a secluded lab beneath the estate here, trying to just understand how this works. There is no cure. They admit that. The best they are hoping for is to ease the symptoms."

She wanted to scream in denial, but her body was burning so hot she couldn't think of anything much past getting his cock out of his pants. The heat was consuming her, making her want, making her need things that brought a flush of humiliation to her entire body.

"Kiowa, it hurts," she finally whispered desperately, flinching as another powerful spasm rippled through her womb.

"What do you want me to do, Amanda?" he whispered. "If I take you, you know what's going to happen. Do you know, when I'm locked inside you, my cock is pressed flush against your cervix, my seed shooting into it. You're ovulating," he reminded her. "Do you want to take that chance again?"

"Do I have a choice?" she screamed back at him, gasping as the anger seemed to build, to feed the sexual desperation climbing within her.

"You have a choice," he snarled in reply. "You can admit you can't run from it, Amanda."

"In less than twenty-four hours you've destroyed every dream I ever had." She was shaking with fury, with lust. "And you expect me to just give up? Oh yes, the great and might Kiowa, king of Coyotes has knotted my cunt, my world is finally right. Damn you, I didn't ask you for this. I didn't ask those bastards to attempt to kidnap me and I didn't ask you to fuck me."

"No, you begged me to," he shot back at her, making her grit her teeth at the memory. "You screamed it, Amanda, you demanded it. And lady, I didn't ask for you any more than you asked for me. At least I have the God-given sense to realize that fighting is a waste of strength."

"I don't belong to you!"

She was screaming. The anger pouring through her was like a spark to the building, surging tide of lusts she couldn't control. She hated it. She needed it more than breath.

"Wrong, baby," he snapped, finally moving toward her, his long-legged stride eating up the short distance, powerful muscles flexing along his upper body, his eyes hot, singeing her. "You do belong to me. Every inch of that sweet, hot little body is mine now. If you don't believe that, try to let another touch you."

She remembered Callan Lyons touching her, catching her as her legs faltered beneath her earlier. The pain had been excruciating.

"You bastard!" she raged.

"Yeah, I am," he agreed as he walked around her, not touching her, letting her smell the intriguing scent of man, honey and spice. "But your bastard it would seem."

She shuddered at the feel of his warmth surrounding her as he passed her on the way to the kitchen.

"God, what a mess." She sighed deeply pushing her fingers roughly through her hair as she watched his lips quirk. Not really a smile, but almost.

"Oh, I don't know," he said softly. "Some things look pretty damned good from where I'm standing. You clean up real fine, Ms. Marion, I have to say that for you."

"I clean up fine?" She rolled her eyes, fighting the arousal as she watched the slow amusement dawn in his eyes. "You are a nutcase. Has anyone mentioned that to you?"

He shrugged powerful muscles. "I think that was Simon's line the night I caught him trying to break into the bar I worked as bouncer for. He wanted to blow the place up. It was my bread-and-butter at the time so I took exception."

"A bouncer?" Oh, her father was going to love this one, but suddenly, it made him seem more real, less of a puppet.

"Yep. Bouncer in a rough-assed brothel/bar called the Raging Lilly just inside this dirty little French town. Filled with terrorists, low-lifes and pond scum. He was itching to blow it to hell and back. Took me a few minutes to convince him of the error of his ways."

"Simon is the guy who drove the jeep?" She fought to concentrate as he handed her a glass of chilled water.

"Drink that. Dehydration is a problem sometimes with these damned matings I was told. And yes, Simon was driving the jeep."

She drank the water, but it did nothing to stem the fever running rampant through her body.

"So, how did you become friends of the Feline Breeds? The last reports I heard, Coyotes were the most feared Breed."

"Not the most feared, the most hated." He shrugged. "Somehow, Simon must have figured out what I was. My best guess is he got a glimpse of that birthmark low on my back. It's a genetic marker of some sort. He was friends with Sinclair, and when he learned the significance of it, he and Sinclair dragged me out of my life of disuse and into this. I'll have to thank him for that. Again."

There was a wry amusement in his gaze. He had a way of making her want to laugh, even when she wanted to hit him with something.

"Kiowa." She licked her dry lips nervously, shaking in the grip of a need so powerful, she knew she was lost to it as he watched her closely. "Please."

He sat his glass then hers on the coffee table, before he moved behind her, his body heat surrounding her.

"Please what, Manda?" he whispered at her ear, his breath wafting over the wound at her neck. "What do you need?"

"You." Stark, blinding, she didn't bother to lie or to deny it to herself any longer. "I need you."

Not conversation, not explanations. His kiss, his touch, the blinding release she knew she was going to find no place but in his arms.

Chapter Sixteen

ഌ

Before she could do more than gasp, Kiowa lifted her in his arms, his lips coming down on hers, his tongue pushing demandingly into her mouth as he carried her to the bedroom.

She wasn't certain how he got the gown off, and she didn't really care. All she cared about was the touch of him, the heat of his body, and the need coursing through her blood.

His lips were on hers, his tongue sharing the intriguing, addictive taste of honey and spice, as he laid her on the bed and came down over her. He was as naked as she. She promised herself that next time, she would figure out how he managed to undress both of them so quickly.

"Don't rush this," he growled as she rubbed against him, stroking her nipples across his chest and gasping at the pleasure of it.

"Me?" she groaned in response. "I'm not the one who has some kind of freaky aphrodisiac pouring out of me. That's your fault."

He grunted at that, a distinctly male sound of frustration that had a smile tugging at her lips. But his eyes crinkled with hidden laughter as he levered himself up to stare down at her, the black centers, despite their heat, soft with tenderness.

"I watched you a week before the kidnapping attempt," he whispered as his hand cupped her cheek. "I followed you to school every morning, I followed you home every evening. If you went out, I was on your ass until you arrived at your destination and back on it until you got home. For a week, I listened to you laugh with your neighbors and coo over their children. And each time I saw you, the need for you grew inside me. No aphrodisiac. Not mating complications. Just a man slowly falling in love with a woman he had no right to."

Her hands tightened on his shoulders as she stared back at him in shock.

"Last night, watching you give those treats out to the kids that came to your door, I was so hard I was about to bust my jeans. I could see so much life in you, so much wonder and joy, that I wanted to snatch you away myself and relish every drop of it. Mating you is no hardship for me, Amanda. But I would have never done this to you, had I known what that kiss would do."

And there was the man. No anger, no regret, simply stating no more than the truth as he saw it. It shouldn't make her heart ache. It shouldn't make her wish for things she knew couldn't be real.

She swallowed the lump that came to her throat and pushed back the tears that would have filled her eyes as her hand moved from his shoulder, her fingers smoothing over his rough velvet lips.

"I'm supposed to be resisting you," she whispered huskily. "You aren't supposed to be the answer to all my sexual fantasies and make my heart ache at the same time, Kiowa."

His brow arched slowly. "The answer to *all* your sexual fantasies?" he asked, the forced playfulness in his voice rending her soul.

He was so strong. Too strong. There were no regrets for who or what he was, no apologies or condemnations for the past. And she couldn't love him, she told herself. She wanted to be a teacher, she wanted her freedom, her independence, didn't she?

"All my sexual fantasies," she finally answered, her voice tight with unshed tears as her body responded to the touch of his.

110

Her hand slid into his hair, her fingertips luxuriating in the cool black silk as his head lowered to hers once again. His tongue painted her lips with a whisper stroke, causing a broken sigh of hunger to escape them.

His hands threaded through her hair as he seemed to relish the taste of her lips and nothing more. He licked them, sipped at them, moaned a deep little growl that came from the depths of his chest and vibrated against her lips.

She watched him, unable to close her eyes or to miss the hungry intent in his expression. This was what she had dreamed of during all those hot nights that arousal stormed her body and wicked wishes pushed at her imagination. Just this.

"Spread your legs for me," he whispered then. "I want to watch your eyes while I fuck you. See the blue darken, the flecks of green lighten. You have such pretty eyes, Amanda."

Her breath hitched in her throat. She spread her thighs slowly, opening herself to him as he moved between them. She could feel his cock, hard and heavy as it lay against the mound of her pussy now, pressing against her clit.

She rolled her hips against him, her breath catching as the steel-hard heat of his erection caressed the sensitive bundle nerves peeking from the folds of her cunt.

"Temptress," he growled, licking her lips again, his eyes locked on hers as he shifted against her, his cock dragging along her sensitive pussy until the thick head was poised at the entrance.

"Are you going to punish me?" She gave him a look of drowsy sensuality, a smile curving her lips as her neck arched, pleasure streaking through her in hard, rapid bolts of heat as he began to push into her.

"Hmm. Punish both of us maybe." He was gritting his teeth now, and Amanda could see the struggle for control that filled his expression.

111

Had it really been less than twenty-four hours since he had first touched her? In that moment, she realized she knew things about Kiowa that she didn't know about her closest acquaintances.

Then he was sliding into her, filling her with a heavy heat and hard strength that stole her thoughts and her mind. She could feel him, stretching her, her muscles protesting in the wake of each hard surge of pre-come that filled her, then eased her. Tingling, curling lashes of sensation assaulted her body as he lay over her, his cock moving slow and inside her, taking her with a gentleness and depth of emotion she didn't want to feel.

She shouldn't feel any emotion. She should feel nothing but the hot grind of their bodies together, his erection sating the unnatural hunger in her body. But she felt more, far deeper than just the depths of her pussy.

With her gaze still locked with his, there was no hiding the pleasure lashing at them both. His expression was feral in its intensity, his eyes so black she felt lost in his gaze. Her body was sensitive, sensitized to him, each rasp of his chest over her hard nipples, his pelvis on her straining clit rocked her to new heights. Each stroke stretched her, filled her, caressed hidden nerves and had her breath catching at the diabolical depth of pleasure building within her.

She rocked beneath him, her legs rising to encase his hips as his lips lowered to hers again. And then her eyes closed. There was no control, no strength to hold them open as he kissed her with a melting passion that left her weak.

With his lips moving on hers, his hips straining against her, driving his cock in harder, faster, sending the bolts of sensation tearing harder through her body, Amanda was lost.

Her back arched as everything inside her exploded. Her body tensed, her pussy tightened around his surging erection until she felt that change, the swelling within her that signaled his own release. It lit a fuse to her already exploding senses and sent her reeling again as she felt his semen jetting inside her.

Long minutes later, she gathered the strength to unlock her legs from his waist and release the hold she had taken on her shoulders. Exhaustion rode her now, as hard as lust had ridden her minutes before.

Her eyes fluttered opened, her vision sleep-blurred as she stared into his dark eyes, sighing in blissful, sated pleasure.

"Sleep, baby," he whispered, resting his head against hers, a restrained shudder working through his body as another pulse of seed filled her milking cunt. "I'll take care of you while you sleep."

Her eyes fluttered closed. She knew that, she thought. He didn't have to say the words. Above all things, she did know Kiowa would take care of her.

Kiowa rarely dreamed. He considered it a blessing. After some of the nightmares of his childhood, he had no desire to visit that inner realm and tempt the angers of the past. But when he drifted into sleep beside Amanda, they were there. Like demons raising their dark, horrifying heads.

"The woman who bore you is dead," his grandfather informed him. "She was killed in a car crash."

Kiowa raised his head from the book he had been devouring. Five. Pitifully thin and small, little else had mattered to him but the words he needed to learn. And learn them he was. He didn't know the woman who bore him, as his grandfather called her. He couldn't even remember her face, though he knew there had been a time that he had been with her.

Kiowa nodded solemnly, staring up at the broad frame of the older man, wishing he could see something other than the twisted expression of distaste that was on his face.

"You don't even care do you?" the old man had growled.

"I don't know her," he had whispered then.

"*That's an animal's response,*" *his grandfather had lashed out.* "*One without a soul.*"

The dream distorted, moved in time. Kiowa was eleven, living alone in the shack high in the mountain, waiting eagerly each week for his grandfather's visit. He knew he had to stay hidden, knew that the people who had forced his birth on the mother he never knew, were searching for him.

The television was his constant companion and with it, he had learned to read over the years, to decipher the words and to make sense of how to use them. Books sat in stacks around the small living room. A blanket was tucked in the couch. He didn't sleep in the bed. In the dark, too many thoughts raced across his mind and too many sounds in the mountains outside fueled his fear.

But that television was his lifeline. On it he saw his dreams. A family. A mother, a father, children who were loved and protected, and in those dreams he could laugh and be free, fly a kite, ride a bike. He didn't have to fear detection.

"*Here's some more books.*" *The box was dumped at his feet as his grandfather stared down at him emotionlessly.*

The other man had gone from disgust to chilly dislike over the years. "*I'll put the food on the porch. You're big enough to put it away yourself.*"

Eleven years old. He had celebrated his birthday alone, clumsily wrapped several pinecones he had found and books he had read in old newspaper and pretended they were a mother's gifts.

"*Thank you, Sir.*" *He had stopped calling him grandfather years before. Grandfathers loved their grandkids. They spoiled them, showed them the world, took them to amusement parks. They didn't lock them away on a mountain and leave them to suffer the silence and the cold alone.*

"*Have you found your soul yet?*" *the old man snapped then.*

Kiowa had stared up at him quietly, years of loneliness and grief locked inside him.

"No, Sir. No soul this week." He had moved slowly past him then and collected the boxes of dry goods and canned foods that he survived on.

Winter was coming on, he could feel it in the air. He wondered if his grandfather would forget to bring him a coat again this year.

Time shifted again. Kiowa had been fourteen the night the news had reported a car crash on the interstate. Joseph Mulligan had been involved in a head-on collision with a semi-truck and killed instantly. He was survived by no remaining family members, the newsman reported. And for the first time in years Kiowa had shed a single tear.

The next day, he packed his meager belongings in a pillowcase and set off down the mountain. Winter was coming again, and the cold was a bitter enemy when you had no dried foods, no warm clothes.

He had read enough and watched enough that he understood certain things where the world was concerned. He knew he had to be careful, that his very creation was a law against nature, the sharp canines that he kept filed down at the side of his mouth were proof of that. He knew there were ways to survive, he just had to be tough enough. Strong enough.

As he walked away from the cabin, he paused and stared back at it quietly.

"I have a soul," he had whispered forlornly. "I always did."

Kiowa's eyes opened slowly, the dream dissipating, but not the woman he held in his arms. Her head lay against his chest, her hair a cloud of silk around their bodies as she slept deeply, peacefully.

He stared to the window, the dark curtain shielding the rays of the sun and tightened his hold on her. If Felines and Wolves mated only once, then there was a chance a Coyote could mate forever as well. He had never wanted another woman as much as he had this one, before he ever touched her. He had never dreamed of another before her, but he had dreamed of this one. He couldn't let her go.

Chapter Seventeen

〜

"Welcome to Sanctuary."

Amanda raised surprised eyes to the front door as it pushed open and Merinus Lyons walked into the cabin. She carried a baby in her arms, the woman behind her carried a foldaway playpen.

"Just put it in the corner, Lilly," Merinus directed the other woman. "We don't want David terrorizing the place while we're here."

Behind her walked an older man, his shoulders stooped, his gray hair mussed. Dark brown eyes regarded her quietly as he sat a large black bag on the living room table. It looked like a doctor's bag.

"I'm Merinus." Her smile was bright, though her brown eyes were shadowed with concern as she turned back to Amanda. "This is Dr. Martins, a very dear friend of mine, and behind him, Serena Grace. She's one of the scientists working within the Feline Breed labs to help find a reason for this mating stuff."

"Hello." Amanda stood still in the kitchen, staring back at them nervously.

Kiowa had left more than an hour ago, leaving her to shower and eat without him. Not that she hadn't been looking forward to a chance to think and to make sense of what was going on.

"I know you have a lot of questions, Amanda," Merinus said gently, her gaze compassionate. "We're here to answer as many as we can, and hopefully manage to steal some blood off you while we're doing it. Callan and Dash said the mating heat is much stronger with you than it has been for the rest of us.

Which is saying something, because trust me, there for a while, it sucked in my case." She laughed freely, her expression self-mocking as she made the statement.

Amanda rubbed her hands slowly up her arms and back down. The thought of being touched by another had her skin crawling.

"It won't be easy," Merinus said gently then. "But what we learn with each case, gives us a greater chance to help others, further down the road."

Amanda stared at the kindly doctor and the scientist that accompanied her.

"What do you need?" she asked as the woman who had set up the playpen and deposited the child in it left the cabin.

"Serena will take vaginal and saliva samples as well as blood. She'll ask you some questions, perform a quick physical then she and Doc will be out of here in no time flat. Then we can talk."

Amanda drew in a deep breath. "When do I get to talk to my father?" She watched Merinus warily.

"Callan is arranging that now," she promised. "We have to be certain of the security on the lines and make certain there's no way anyone can tap the conversation. Keeping you safe is our highest priority, Amanda."

Amanda swallowed tightly, her gaze flickering to the aristocratic features of the scientist and the weary sympathy in the doctor's.

"Fine. Let's get it over with," she breathed out roughly.

"Ms. Marion, the samples needed and the examination won't come without its discomfort," Dr. Grace warned, her voice soft, her gray eyes worried. "The mating heat creates several different hormones that we've been able to identify and isolate. One of them is extreme sensitivity to any touch other than the mate's. Surgical gloves aid in that, but the body chemistry doesn't take long to identify the fact that an alien presence is touching it. It reacts with pain."

"Yeah. Been there, done that," Amanda muttered wearily. "Let's just get it the hell over with. This is starting to get on my nerves."

It wasn't helping that she needed Kiowa. You would think she would be fucked dry, Amanda thought cynically. Instead, she was damned near as willing and eager as she had been the first time.

"The good news is, that the body slowly adjusts to the hormones," Serena revealed. "After this, if you follow the same pattern as Merinus, Roni, Sherra and Elizabeth, then you'll see a reduction in the heat and its symptoms until ovulation reoccurs."

Amanda blinked back at the scientist in amazement before turning to Merinus.

"It never goes away?" she asked, horrified.

Merinus' lips tilted in amusement. "Not completely. But it's really not that bad. Makes for some wicked bedtime stories," she finished with a throaty laugh.

"This is a nightmare," Amanda sighed, pushing her fingers through her hair as she stared back at the scientist. "Fine, let's just get it over with."

"We'll use the bedroom." The scientist picked up the bag the doctor had carried in and followed Amanda into the bedroom.

It was horrifying. An hour later Amanda was sweating profusely, agony racing through her body as she forced back her cries and endured first the vaginal exam and collecting of fluid samples from the agonized channel. The breast exam had her biting her lip until she tasted blood. It felt like needles—no, knives—were being plunged into her shrinking flesh as the scientists hands examined them carefully.

Finally, her gown covering her modestly, she sat on the edge of the bed, tears pouring down her cheeks as Dr. Grace snapped a rubber tie around her upper arm and began to prepare the vein for the extraction of blood.

She hurt. God, she had never hurt like this. Every cell, every nerve ending in her body was screaming against the touch as she forced her cries back in her throat. She watched the needle coming close to her skin, her eyes wide, seeing almost in slow motion as the sharp point came closer and closer to contact. Her body was rioting, her stomach twisting with the pain.

A second before it made contact, a broad hand clamped over the scientist's wrist and a violent, enraged growl echoed around them. Amanda followed the hand to the arm, up to broad shoulders to the black, furious eyes of the man staring down at them.

"Kiowa." Merinus entered the room behind him. "It's not as bad as it looks."

He turned his head, his black hair flowing over his shoulder as his lips curled back in a snarl and he growled again. An animalistic possessive sound that even Amanda had no intention of protesting.

The needle dropped from the scientist's hand as she stared at Amanda in shock.

"Get the fuck away from her," he ordered harshly, drawing the other woman back slowly. "Get your needles and your samples, pack up and leave. Now. Come back without my permission and I'll kill you."

He meant it. Amanda could see it in the tense lines of his body, the fury emanating from his voice.

"And you accuse me of being childish," she said in amazement as the doctor moved away quickly, massaging her wrist as she kept a careful eye on Kiowa.

"You are being foolhardy," he snapped, swinging his gaze back to her. "Why suffer this way? Why would you allow yourself to be hurt in such a manner?"

"They need the information," she argued back. "Dammit, Kiowa, someone has to find a cure."

He recoiled as though she had smacked him. She watched the mask drop into place, the blank eyes, the emotionless expression. She shivered at the look, knowing that somehow she had just made him angrier than he already was. No, she had hurt him. That stark, blinding truth whipped through her mind and had her staring back at him in surprise. Somehow, she had hurt him.

"Merinus, tell your mate I'll return to the communications shed later," he finally said quietly, never looking at her.

"We need those blood samples, Kiowa," Merinus said firmly. "We're almost finished."

"No. You are finished. Not almost." His voice was too soft, too dangerously controlled. "Leave now, Merinus."

He was exceedingly polite but Amanda swore she could feel murder in the air.

Amanda rose slowly to her feet as the room cleared out.

"This is my choice," she told him coldly. "Not yours."

He stood stiffly in front of her for one long moment before turning away from her.

"Are you hungry? I thought I would fix us dinner. Your father should be calling in a few hours. I think I should warn you, though; Callan has a ban on information concerning the mating heat. It's the one thing you cannot mention to him."

She stared at his back in shock.

"No, damn you," she cursed furiously. "You will not pull that I-feel-nothing-change-the-subject routine on me. We'll discuss what I can and cannot say to my father later." She gripped his arm just inside the living room pulling him to a stop as he turned back to her slowly. "This was my choice. My decision. You had no right to take it from me."

"I'm your mate. It's within all my rights to protect you. Even from yourself."

"From myself?" She lifted her brows in amazement, her hands fisting at her side to keep from knocking him over the head with something. "I wasn't trying to commit suicide. It was just an examination."

"Which caused you excessive pain." He could have been discussing the weather. *Oh, by the way, the sun was shining today but I think it was a bit overbright,* she thought sarcastically.

"My pain," she snapped. "Dammit, Kiowa, they will never figure this out without the tests. Without someone willing to endure them. Do you think this is comfortable for me? That I enjoy having my very will stolen from me in such a way?"

"The heat eases." He shrugged dismissively, pulling away from her. No emotion. Nothing.

"That doesn't help when it's burning you alive," she informed him furiously. "And that's besides the fact it was none of your business. It was my choice."

"Then make another choice. "

"'Then leave again."

He stopped at the entrance to the kitchen, his shoulders flexing beneath the light gray shirt he wore.

"I think I'll stay, thank you." he finally said mildly.

Amanda shook her head as amazement cascaded along her senses.

"Do you think I'm just going to accept this, Kiowa?" she finally asked him softly, knowing she never would.

"I really don't think you have a choice. Now we need to discuss your father and what you cannot say." He stared back at her unblinking then, and for a moment she wondered if he did have a soul.

Chapter Eighteen

𝕤𝕠

She refused to just accept.

Amanda made her way as quietly as possible from the cabin, staying in the shadows as she forced herself to move into the darkness of the mountain the cabin sat within.

She had listened to Kiowa, Kane Tyler and Callan Lyons discussing the security of the compound earlier, before Kiowa left to help Kane with some kind of computer malfunction. After she had talked to her father and reassured him she was fine. Not that she could do anything else with Kiowa standing over her like an avenging angel. She had even whispered their code phrase—*I'm fine, Poppa*—rather than Father...and she still couldn't explain to herself why she had done that.

Perhaps because the independence she had won from her family had been so very hard to achieve. Her father and brother were just waiting on the excuse to haul her back into the fold, marry her to a nice, staid, dependable young man and see her become the perfect Washington wife.

She didn't think so. Fighting it out with Kiowa would be easier. And she was about to show him here and now that she wasn't someone he could so casually order around. She would get herself off this damned mountain, out of the Breed Compound and back to the White House on her own. It wouldn't be so difficult. By rescuing herself, she could assert her independence even in the face of the danger surrounding her.

Escape wouldn't be that hard. All she had to do was hit the old logging road and head to the county road several miles away.

She could flag a car down, get a ride to the nearest phone and call her father. He wouldn't have left her in the Breeds' care if he had known the truth. And she knew Kiowa was desperate to keep that truth hidden until he could convince her to accept the mating as it stood.

She snorted at that as she sprinted past the clearing at the back of the house and headed into the tree line. Nature could get as ugly as it wanted to. Amanda hadn't chosen Kiowa, and having the choice forced on her wasn't her idea of a perfect relationship.

There had to be a way to cure it. A way to make the heat go away and give her a chance to decide for herself the man she wanted.

Would she have chosen Kiowa if she had a choice? Her body screamed yes, her heart ached.

Love didn't come in a day, did it? No matter what she had read or how she had fantasized, she knew reality was a different matter entirely. Kiowa was a loner, a Coyote Breed, bred to manipulate and to deceive. But didn't humans, whether Breed or not, do those very same things?

Confusion was a morass of thoughts and feelings inside her head that she couldn't make sense of. Couldn't control. Fear was as overriding as the building arousal, and safety could only be found in the normal. She needed to go home. She had to talk to Alexander. As coldly furious as he would get, he would help her.

She stumbled through the forest, the long flannel shirt she wore snagging on the brush she passed. The jeans and sneakers protected her from the chill in the air, but nothing could protect her from the internal heat. It was building. She had prayed that by separating herself from Kiowa and the scent that seemed to fill the cabin that she could survive the need.

She would survive it, she told herself fiercely. All she had to do was get home.

Clouds moved slowly over the night sky, dimming the moonlight and increasing the darkness of the forest. Dammit, she hated the dark. This was why she lived in the city rather than her father's estate in upper Pennsylvania.

It wasn't that she was scared of the dark; she just didn't like it. It was filled with sounds she couldn't identify, sounds that sent chills up her spine and made her think of every horror movie Alexander had ever dared her to watch.

The scream of a cat, a big cat, echoed through the mountain now. She paused, breathing roughly, her eyes wide as she attempted to see through the darkness. Okay, what was it Kiowa said? If you didn't smell like a cat, they would eat you.

Oh God. This was just great. Wild wolves and big cats, a mating heat that was making her crazy and God only knew what else was coming. She didn't need any of this.

She moved faster, no longer worrying about silence or stealth. What the hell was the point?

"Kane, we have unauthorized movement in Sector Three C," the female Breed communications expert, Tamber, reported quietly as Kane and Kiowa worked on the quirky program they were trying to install to intercept web traffic from blood supremacist members.

Kiowa's head came up, his eyes narrowing. Three C was the area the small cabin he and Amanda were using was located.

"There's no electronic indicator and the cats are heading that way."

"Fuck!" Kiowa came quickly to his feet. "It's Amanda. Call them back."

He should have known her easy capitulation earlier that night had been no more than a ruse. He had smelled her fury, her sense of betrayal at his refusal to allow the tests or to explain why.

How was he supposed to tell her that the sight of her enduring such pain stripped him of pride and nearly brought tears to his eyes? That his chest had tightened and rage like nothing he had never known had filled his mind?

"Have Dawn's unit intercept," Kane ordered quickly. "We're heading there now."

He threw Kiowa one of the comm units they used as he attached his own to his ear.

"Dawn is moving to intercept, Cabal and Tanner are joining for animal control. The cats have been restless, Kane. They might not obey standard commands," the young female Breed at the communications table reported.

"Have Merc ready the cycles," he snapped back at her. "We're heading out."

Kiowa tensed as he followed Kane at a run, fury building in his mind with each damned second. Damn her, he hadn't expected her to run. How had she had the energy to run?

"The cycles will make quick work of the distance," Kane yelled as they approached the sound of powerful motors revving inside a metal shed on the other side of the compound.

"I'm going to beat her," Kiowa muttered. "Dammit to hell. I warned her."

"Goddammit, Kiowa," Kane cursed as they burst into the well lit shed, the wide doors shoved open. "How easy do you think this is on her? We should have expected it."

But they hadn't, and because of his lack of foresight, Amanda was in danger.

They jumped on the readied, powerful little cycles. Built for speed and mountain runs, the motorcycles were specially designed by Mercury, the towering lion breed who oversaw their care like a mother hen.

They shot from the shed at full throttle, spinning recklessly as they took a sharp turn around the driveway that led to the shed and headed up the graveled road into the mountain.

"She's made it more than a mile from the cabin," Kane yelled into the comm link. "Heading for the main road. Cats are moving in fast so let's make this quick."

The big cats were getting closer. She could hear their throttled screams echoing around her as though calling out to each other, working in coordination to track her down.

Amanda was running, stumbling over brush and logs as she fought to keep from falling and rolling down the mountain. God only knew what lay at the bottom of some of the ravines she had detected.

She was fighting to breathe as fear raced through her body and her own weakness slapped her in the face. Surely it would have been easier to steal a cell phone. She wouldn't be eaten at any rate.

She tripped over something. Her own feet maybe as another savage feline scream sounded behind her. Landing on her stomach, she struggled to get back to her feet, coming to her knees and then eyeball to eyeball with the biggest meanest-looking lion she had ever laid her eyes on.

He roared. Opened his powerful jaws, displaying a mouthful of razor-sharp teeth and roared right in her face.

"I taste really bad," she snapped, too scared to try to move as he leveled that eerie amber stare at her. "And I don't have any meat on my bones. Dad is always telling me I'm too damned skinny... I bet rabbits taste really good..." she whimpered. "Oh God, go find a rabbit."

He growled, lifting his lip and displaying the brutal teeth at the side of his mouth. His head was huge, the thick mane that grew from the back of it indicating a mature, able creature in his prime.

"He doesn't care much for rabbits. His favorite treats are dumb little girls who like to disregard measures set up for their own safety."

The female voice had her jerking around, only to earn her a sharp nip on her back from the animal at her back.

She jerked back around, staring in surprise as he roared again.

"Can you call him off or something?" she gasped. The little bite hadn't hurt, but she would prefer not to have a chunk taken out of her.

"Tiny pretty much does what he wants," the woman drawled softly, her voice soft, almost melodic as she came around Amanda and hunched down beside the animal. "Don't you, Tiny?"

The lion butted against the woman, her features too dim and Amanda's gaze too filled with sharp teeth to pay much attention to how she looked.

The huge animal made a soft snuffling sound as he rubbed against the woman's leg, obviously content for the moment.

"Good boy." She stroked his mane and then amazingly enough, purred with a kittenish soft sound. "Go lay down and I'll talk to our visitor a minute. Tanner will be here soon with your treat."

The lion's head swung back to Amanda, the look he gave her one of pure male aggravation, but he turned and moved a few inches away, plopping down on the ground and watching her closely.

"I can't connect with them very well," the woman kept her voice pitched to that melodic, almost mesmerizing tone. "Just stay quiet and nice and unthreatening and he should be fine until Tanner and Cabal arrive. They're right behind me."

Amanda wasn't taking her eyes off the lion.

"Was I close?" she asked, her voice barely above a breath.

"Not even close," she sighed. "Actually, another twenty feet or so in this direction is a hidden ravine. You might not have survived the fall."

Amanda lowered her head dejectedly.

"Is it so bad?" the woman asked her then, her voice reflective. "My sister mated with Kane, he's not a Breed, but he should have been one. Is the mating horrible?"

Amanda flicked a surprised look to the dark form. Still kneeling on hands and knees, she was terrified to move. The lion wasn't taking his eyes off her.

"Umm. No," she said carefully.

The mating was great. The dumb male that thought he was suddenly her lord and master was beginning to suck though.

"Then why are you running?" A dark head tilted, pale features barely discernable in the darkness as she stayed hunched between Amanda and the animal. "Kiowa is the most honorable Coyote I've known. He's not like the jailors we had, trained to mercilessness. He has the scent of truth, of gentleness. Why are you running from him? Are human males more worthy?"

Amanda blinked back at the other woman in amazement. Her voice was soft, somber, as though the question held more importance than she wanted to let on.

"How the hell should I know?" She swallowed tightly. "Look, this is really weird. Can you tell that monster to let me sit down?"

The monster growled.

"I would really stay still a few more seconds," the woman advised. "I can smell Tanner and Cabal approaching. They'll come in easily to keep from upsetting the cats. There are several around us you know. My lionesses will try to protect you if Tiny attacks, but I would prefer they not be hurt. And you didn't answer my question."

"Ask me when I'm not about to become a lion snack," Amanda suggested.

She chuckled. "I was merely curious. Perhaps you were right to run. Sex isn't a pleasant act." Her voice was filled with shadows then. "A mating could be no better."

"He doesn't hurt me," Amanda had no idea why it mattered that the woman know that.

Amber eyes, much like the lion's, regarded her quietly.

"I've heard you scream."

Amanda could feel the flush heating her body further.

"Yeah, well. Sometimes screaming is good." She cleared her throat nervously. "This is a really weird conversation, you know?"

"I understand." The other woman's head nodded before she rose carefully and spoke again. "Tanner, Tiny is more upset than usual. This woman's scent isn't the one bothering him, but he's becoming more agitated by the night."

"What of your lionesses?" The male voice was as carefully soft as the female's.

Amanda had only a vague impression of sliding darkness, a shadow that passed by her. No sound heralded the stranger's arrival until the lion began to purr roughly. Darkness shielded the animal then, only to be joined by another form.

"They can't find the disturbance," she reported, her hand gripping Amanda's arm and urging her up as the sound of motorcycles grew nearer.

"He's settled for now," the man she had called Tanner said softly before crooning to the animal again.

"Shit," Amanda whispered as the throb of the cycles began to shatter the night. "Kiowa's coming, isn't he?"

"Yes. Kiowa is coming." A slender hand tightened on her arm. "If he's hurting you, I can help you Amanda. Don't lie to me."

"Dawn," the man behind her said warningly. "This is none of your concern. Kiowa has the right to his mate. You know this."

"Not if he hurts her," her voice deepened. "I and my lionesses will protect you, Amanda, if he's hurting you."

"Goddammit, Dawn..." A rough curse, but one filled with pain, not anger filled the night. "Seth won't hurt you."

Amanda shook her head in confusion. There was more going on here than this strange woman's concern.

"He doesn't hurt me..." The motorcycles lit up the area as they slid around the bend, coming to a bone-jarring stop that had the lion on his feet, a roar ripping through the night as a dozen women stepped from the trees and surrounded the nervous lion.

"Amanda, I'm going to paddle your ass," Kiowa's voice was furious, hot.

Amanda's buttocks clenched at the thought. And it wasn't in fear.

She watched him swing from the motorcycle, broad, muscular, his expression dark and forbidding, his black eyes glittering with hunger and anger as he strode to her. Her pussy wept as he neared, her womb clenched spasmodically as her thighs tightened in reflex.

He would have drawn her even in a more civilized setting. He would have starred in her fantasies, he would have been a man she would have gravitated to, heedless of his genetic makeup.

In that moment, she realized it might not be love, but it could have been. Would he have courted her? Hell no, he would have barreled right over her, just as he did now. He would have taken her and made her love it, and her cunt would have wept at his touch, even without the fire burning her alive now.

He stopped in front of her, staring down at her with brutal, naked lust.

"Do I need to tie you down?" he snapped then, the fury burning in him echoing in his voice.

Amanda smoothed her hands down her jeans and stared up at him as she admitted to herself that just as he had said, there would be no escaping him.

"Will you still spank me?"

He blinked. Once. Then narrowed his eyes on her.

"That's a given," he growled.

"Might as well go for broke." She shrugged then. "What's a few ropes into the bargain?"

"Let's go." He gripped her arm, his hand wrapping around hers like the gentlest vise as he pulled her to the motorcycle. "Payback time, baby. Let's see how you like a different kind of throb between your thighs."

Chapter Nineteen

୨୬

Unfortunately, she climaxed on the ride back to the cabin. Amanda was begging at that point, because the release did nothing to ease her, it only made her hotter. She knew what her body wanted. Knew what it craved.

"Kiowa, please…" she cried out as he pulled her from the cycle and forced her to walk to the cabin door.

Every jarring motion to her body was torturous pleasure. Her nerves were rioting, screaming out for his touch, his kiss, begging for ease. As the door slammed behind him, he turned, pushed her against it and slammed his lips to hers.

Yes. Her mouth opened for his tongue before closing on it, drawing it, groaning at the heady taste that filled her senses and the pleasure that stormed her body. She arched to him, rubbing against his heat and strength as his hands buried in her hair, holding her still for the kiss that locked them together.

Her hands weren't still. She had waited too long, the throb of the powercycle between her legs had been like throwing gas to a bonfire. She was burning out of control. Buttons popped from his shirt, if she wasn't mistaken material tore as she fought to get to bare male flesh.

All the while, his tongue was pumping into her mouth, his heated growl stroking her senses as his thumb moved to caress the wound at her neck. She cried out into the kiss, as the subtle stroking motion of his thumb sent riotous fire streaking through her.

His jeans were next. Her hands slid down his heaving chest, his taut abdomen, until she could jerk at the snap at the waistband of his jeans. Nothing mattered but touching him, being filled by him.

"Not yet, you little witch," he snarled as he caught her hands, jerking them above her head and anchoring them with one of his big hands.

She opened her eyes languorously, staring back at him in drowsy passion as she licked the taste of him from her lips.

"Are you going to spank me?" She couldn't get the thought of it out her head.

A wicked smile tilted his lips as he watched her with dark lust.

"I should tie you down and let you suffer," he retorted. "Let you see the agony coming, Amanda, if you actually manage to leave me. That would serve you right."

"You're killing me, Kiowa." She strained toward him. "Threaten me later, fuck me now."

He growled, a low warning sound that had chills of pleasure racing up her spine.

"You're pushing your luck."

"Then spank me and show me the error of my ways." She rubbed her breasts across his bared chest, gasping at the sweet pleasure of her shirt rasping the sensitive little nubs.

His hand tightened on her wrists as the other hand moved from her head to the front of her shirt. A second later the sound of material rending nearly had her climaxing. Who knew it could be that sexy, having the clothes torn from her body in such a way?

"Kick off your shoes." His voice was a hard, warning hiss of lust and danger.

His black eyes were gleaming with hunger, his cheeks flushed with it, lips kiss-swollen and heavy with sensuality.

Amanda kicked her shoes off slowly, using her toes to nudge the footwear off before kicking it away.

The smell of sex, sweet and heavy, filled the air. Her arousal, his, they mingled to create a scent addictive and overpowering to the senses.

His free hand went to her jeans then, pulling apart the snap before jerking the zipper down. His hand pushed into the opened flap as a ragged groan tore from her lips.

His fingers slid between her thighs, two moving through her slit to tease the entrance to her pussy.

"You're so wet you're about to soak those jeans." He leaned forward, his lips settling on the wound at her neck before his tongue licked over it.

"Kiowa. This is cruel," she whimpered as she strained against him, desperate for a deeper, harder touch.

"You'll learn not to disobey me, Amanda." He sounded stern, dominant. A rush of juices flooded his fingers as she gasped at the pleasure his voice brought, the thrill of defying him and enduring his punishment.

A breath of mocking laughter sounded at her ear. "You think the pleasure will compensate for the punishment," he asked her softly, his teeth tugging at her earlobe. "That a Breed male doesn't understand how to make his woman submit, Manda? Do you think nature didn't allow for such female stubbornness?"

She bit her lip, shuddering in his grip then. She was straining in excitement, her oversensitive body so aroused she knew it would take very little to send her careening over the edge.

His hand slid back, his fingers caressing from the entrance of her vagina to the straining nub of her clitoris but never giving her enough for satisfaction. Before she could guess his intentions he released her wrists, only to pick her up and carry her to the sofa.

Moving faster than she, with her dazed senses could struggle, he had her jeans stripped from her body before flipping her over his lap.

"Kiowa." She howled his name when his hand landed on the upraised cheeks of her ass.

It burned with a fire that shot straight to her pussy.

His hand landed again on the other cheek a second before his fingers dipped between her thighs, spearing through the thick juices that lay on her cunt and spreading them back.

"There." His voice was hard, thick with hunger as he massaged the delicate opening to her anus a second before the third slap was delivered.

Amanda jerked against him, crying out in pleasure as she felt the tingling warmth whip through her body.

Once again, his fingers moved to her pussy, dipping into the unlimited well of cream that spilled from her body and drawing it back. This time, his fingertip sank into the tight entrance of her anus.

She writhed across his lap, fire spreading from nerve ending to nerve ending as she screamed his name.

"Stay still." He tapped her ass again, a bit harder in warning, but it only served to drive her deeper into the sexual madness consuming her.

"Do you know how pretty you are?" he asked her roughly, his fingers dipping into her pussy again. "Your ass is turning a soft, soft pink, parting for me, giving me a clear view of this..."

His finger sank into her tighter entrance again as he pulled her cheeks further apart, opening her, straining the muscles that clenched him.

He pulled back, his finger slipping free, only to deliver another sharp caress to the rounded curves of her butt. It was thrilled, pleasure-pain, an incredible feast of the senses that Amanda knew, that mating heat or not, she could have never resisted.

Kiowa's calloused hand was sensually rough, the short, sharp smacks to her tender flesh burning through her sanity and making her wild, making her desperate. She needed him now. Needed his cock filling her, burning through her pussy as she erupted with pleasure.

Then his fingers moved back to the wellspring of slick juices easing from her, drawing them back, lubricating the little hole between her buttocks so his finger could sink deeper inside her.

She was impaled there again, fighting the unfamiliar penetration as her senses luxuriated in it. Fire bloomed in her anus, spread through her loins and wrapped around her straining clit. Then it was gone. She cried out, her hips bucking, pitching back as she fought to keep from begging for more.

His hand landed on her rear again. Several sharp, stinging smacks that drove her close to the edge of release, leaving her teetering on the precipice and begging for more. Just a little more. Just enough to pitch her over.

"Kiowa please…" she begged long seconds later, her butt burning, her pussy in flames as he paused to smooth his hand over the sensitive flesh.

"Please what, Amanda?" he asked her, his voice dark and seductive. "Please don't touch you? Please don't pleasure you?"

"No," she wailed. "Kiowa please, it's killing me."

His finger sank into the tight little hole again, causing her to press back to him, to drive him deeper inside her as her pussy rippled in impending orgasm.

"Do you think it's going to be that easy, baby?" he asked her, his crooning tone all the more savage for the dark sexuality in his voice.

He pulled back before thrusting inside her again, moving his finger easily in the juices that now lubricated the tight channel. Amanda tried to spread her legs wide, to gain enough support to thrust back, to intensify the friction.

He chuckled at her efforts before pulling free once again and setting her on her feet. Or trying to. Her knees were weak, her senses tuned too deeply to the sensual fires burning in her body so that he had no choice but to lift her in his arms as he stood up and strode to the bedroom.

He tossed her onto the wide mattress, staring down at her with devil's black eyes as he loosened his jeans. Leaving the material gaping at the front, giving her only a glimpse of his straining cock, he moved to the closet. When he turned back to her, she shivered at the sight of the ropes in his hands.

"You think it's going to be so easy, don't you, baby?" he asked her as he bound her arms, then her legs, leaving more slack in the bonds than she had expected. "You think I'm going to drive you over the edge and have to deal with you running again?"

"I won't run." She could barely talk, let alone consider leaving him again. "I promise."

She had decided that while staring into the lion's eyes. Kiowa would learn, later, that she wasn't the only one who was going to obey.

"You promised before," he growled. "What did you do, cross your fingers the first time?"

She nodded desperately. Whatever it would take to get his cock inside her, she would do at this point.

"Not that easy." The smile that curved his lips gave her a glimpse of the wicked canines at the side of his mouth and had her shoulder throbbing sharply in response to the thought of how easily he had driven her to madness when he pierced her flesh with them.

She licked her lips nervously.

"Uh-uh." He shook his head at her as he came to his knees on the bed. "Don't lick your lips, baby, lick this."

She opened for the flared, angrily flushed head of his cock. Her tongue curled over it, licked as her lips closed and she sucked it deep inside her mouth. The pre-come spurted instantly into her mouth. Honey sweet, spicy. She moaned, her eyes closing then opening quickly as the fingers of one hand captured a nipple and gripped firmly.

She shuddered in pleasure, moaning around his cock as she began to suckle at it frantically. It was thick, wide, filling her mouth and her senses with a male strength just as addictive as the mating heat was.

"God, that's good," he whispered, pulling back then thrusting easily between her lips again. "So sweet and hot, Manda."

She stared up at him, seeing something in his eyes she didn't want to acknowledge. An emotion, a depth that snared her and bound her tighter than any ropes created.

She drew on him, her tongue swiping over the head as he retreated, her moans filling the room as he returned, her pleasure echoing around them with each small spurt of pre-come that filled her mouth.

She was lost, and she admitted it. Hopelessly bound to this man and unable to escape. Her mouth tightened further as she arched to his touch, dying for the pleasure that whipped through her body, that made her blood sing in ecstasy.

"Enough," he groaned, pulling back from her lips, his eyes narrowing in dark promise as he lowered himself beside her.

"I know what you like," he whispered. "But how long can you bear it?"

Chapter Twenty

ജ

Kiowa had passed rage when he learned she had run. Pure fear had filled him, a part of his soul shattering at the thought of never touching her, never tasting her soft flesh again. She had, in a few short days, become every breath he took. The instinctive part of his brain had screamed out in denial, the human part of his soul had raged in pain.

When he found her, kneeling in the dirt, that fucking lion no more than feet from her and wary as a caged beast, he knew then that he would have to do something, anything to convince her that life without him would break them both.

So he used what he had. The pleasure he could give her. The heat that consumed her, and that little edge of pain he knew that made her senses skyrocket and her body convulse in release.

What it did to him was just as amazing. Never had he known so much pleasure from simply the giving of it. The arch of her body, the glaze of perspiration over her skin, the sound of her husky cries echoing around them. It made each touch, each whisper of skin over skin more arousing than the most experienced touch he had ever received.

Driving her higher was all that mattered. Tasting her, pleasuring her, was his only concern.

And damn if she didn't taste good. His lips moved from breast to breast, suckling soft, hard, his tongue lashing at her peaked nipple as he stared up at her, watching as she slipped deeper and deeper in the sheer sexuality of the act.

She was coming apart in his arms, and he loved it.

As his mouth continued to torture and torment her tight little nipples he smoothed one hand along her inner thigh, feeling it tense as he came closer to the scalding heat of her pussy.

His fingers slid through the shallow slit, a groan escaping his throat at the strangled scream that tore from her. She was honey sweet, hot enough to singe his senses, her heated scent making his mouth water for just a taste.

As he reached the engorged bud of her clit, he lifted his hand then patted the swollen mound firmly. Her hips reared up as screaming pleas filled the bedroom.

"Oh God, Kiowa, I swear. I swear..." she cried. "I won't run again. I swear. Please do something..."

"But I am doing something." He was panting for breath, consumed by a hunger for her he had no desire to deny.

He patted her sensitive pussy again, knowing it would take very little to set off the throbbing trigger of her clit. She was so ready to come that even her pussy trembled with the need.

"Kiowa..." her voice dropped to a trembling, breathless cry. "I swear. I swear..."

"Shhh, baby," he whispered, his mouth moving from her breasts to her damp abdomen and then lower. "Just enjoy it, Manda. Just let me make you feel good."

His tongue circled her throbbing clit, the taste of her going to his head like the most potent drug. She was so sweet, so liquid hot and slick it was like plunging his tongue in melted sugar when he thrust it up the velvet confines of her cunt.

He knew what he was going to do. Not that he had planned it, or even really considered it until she had run from him. The moment he had realized she had entered the mountain and placed herself in greater danger, Kiowa had known exactly how he would imprint her submission to him in her mind, her heart.

She was his mate. She was falling in love with him, he could see it in her eyes, feel it in her touch. She would come to realize that her heart as well as her body was bound to him. But until she did, she would learn his word was law where her protection was concerned. She was not strong enough to protect herself. She had no idea of the depravity of the world and those who would take her from him if they had a chance. He would not give them the chance, and neither would she.

As his lips moved back to her straining clitoris, he plunged two fingers quickly into the weeping depths of her pussy. She exploded fast, arching and shuddering as her cries filled his ears.

He gave her only seconds to peak and begin the gentle slide down before he moved away. Before she had the will or the mind to fight him, he loosened the restraints and flipped her quickly to her stomach.

She gasped as he allowed his hand to fall to the smooth, rounded globes of her ass again. Damn she was pretty there, her flesh still pink from the earlier spanking, the small entrance to her anus flexing in response to the orgasm slowly easing through her body.

He lifted her hips, bracing her knees on the bed.

"Stay," he growled when she would have lain back down. "On your knees, just like that."

Her legs tightened as she whimpered, arousal still thick in her voice.

"You will not endanger yourself like that again, Amanda," he snarled, his hands moving to position her knees on the bed as he wanted them, angling her hips back, her rosy rear parting to reveal the ultra-tight entrance to her ass.

"Do you know what I'm going to do, Manda?" he asked her softly, crooning, his voice deepening at the thought of the pleasure to come.

"Just do it," she cried out, her buttocks flexing.

He chuckled at the demand, moving his fingers along her saturated pussy to spread the honeyed lubrication back to the little hole.

He slid his finger in slowly, watching as it stretched her asshole, feeling his breath catch in his throat as she relaxed easily for him. He eased her slowly, one finger stretching and feeling her, then two, then three. At the third, she was gasping, her back bowing as her strangled cries echoed around him.

Moving his fingers back, he edged closer, tucking the thick head of his dick at the tender opening.

"Kiowa…" Her voice was drugged, sensual as he pressed close, feeling the hard pulse of fluid that exited the tip at the feel of the tight entrance.

Instinct, Dash had told him. A biological, instinctive response to the female's tight channels and the unusual thickness of the wolf and coyote breeds. Their dicks were unusually thick, though not abnormal. Without it, he could have never attempted what he knew he was going to do now. Hell, he had never attempted if before, had never known it would be possible.

"Kiowa." Amanda pressed closer, her voice breathy, dazed with the arousal straining through her.

He had only kissed her once, deliberately. He wanted to stroke the fires of her lust, not the hormone that spilled from his tongue. He wanted to make her crazy, his touch, her need for it, driving her.

His cock spurted again as he pressed deeper. She cried out as the fluid shot into tight, tense muscles.

"Talk to me, baby," he groaned, hanging onto his control by a thread. "Tell me if you want it, Amanda."

"Yes." The harsh groan had his teeth gritting as he pressed deeper.

"Damn. You're tight," he panted, feeling the grip, tighter than any fist stretching around the head of his cock.

"Kiowa…" The low drawn-out wail as more of the relaxing fluid shot into her had his head falling back on his neck, his grip on her hips tightening.

The very fact that she was accepting, allowing the penetration was proof of her trust, the intimacy growing between them. Amanda was as prickly as a porcupine protecting its lair; she would never give such liberties without complete trust.

"You will not endanger yourself again." He pushed deeper, the head of his erection popping inside the stretched muscles now as she flexed around him, causing yet another hard surge of the hormonal fluid inside her tight ass. "Never, Amanda."

"I swear," she cried hoarsely. "Oh God, Kiowa, I can't bear it."

He pulled back, easing from her immediately, only to have her scream in denial and push back, lodging him deeper inside her.

"What do you want, Amanda?" he demanded fiercely. "Tell me what you want."

"You..." She was gasping for breath, shuddering each time his cock pulsed inside her. "I want you."

"Not good enough," he snapped. "Tell me what you want, Amanda. Tell me now or I'll stop."

"No!" She pressed closer, moving back against him, pushing him deeper inside her as she screamed out at the sensations.

"Tell me!" His hand landed on her ass demandingly.

"Fuck me," she snarled, her voice slurred, enraptured. "Damn you, fuck my ass, Kiowa. Fuck me."

Two hard blistering jets of the pre-come surged from his cock a second later. Kiowa pushed deeper, gritting his teeth, holding her tight as she writhed beneath him until every tortured, engorged inch of his dick was buried inside her.

She was crying now, her muscles flexing and rippling around him, fighting to accommodate the flesh filling her.

"Mine!" He couldn't stop the growl that barreled from his throat as he came over her, his lips searching for the tender wound he had left on her neck as he felt his release building in his balls.

She was too tight, too hot around him, and despite the thick lubrication his cock had spurted inside her and his normally steely self-control, he knew he wouldn't last but seconds. She was closer. He could smell it. Feel her pussy rippling through the walls of her ass and knew when he knotted the delicate portal he was lodged in, her orgasm might well destroy them both.

"Yes!" Her uninhibited scream shocked him, renewed him. "God yes, Kiowa. Yours. Yours. Now fuck me, damn you."

She tightened on him again, her anus flexing, rippling until he had no choice. He was moving inside her, long thrusts that he fought to keep gentle, to keep from hurting her, but her cries urged him on, drove him insane.

His hands were tight on her hips as she followed each stroke, the sound of smacking flesh and wet sex filling the air until he knew he couldn't bear it any longer. He prayed Dash had known what the hell he was talking about, because Kiowa couldn't have pulled from her now if both their lives depended on it.

He thrust hard and deep, feeling it happen, the tightness halfway up his cock, the sudden swelling as his balls tightened and his cock hardened further. It was exquisite, the most pleasure he could have known in his life.

The first hard rush of semen came as he felt her inner walls stretching, allowing the knot to press into her pussy as it stretched the anal wall, to throb hard and deep inside her, pushing her over an edge unfamiliar to her if her screams were any indication. Throttled, weak sounds interspersed with his name, her vows, her sweet voice swearing she would never run again.

His. Always his.

His teeth bit into her, even though he had sworn to deny himself that pleasure. This time, there was no blood, only sweet, giving female flesh beneath his laving tongue and her soft voice urging him on.

He filled her with his semen, jerking above her, feeling the hard pulse of her release as well, and knowing at that moment, if she ever left him, if he ever lost her, he would be only half a man. His soul would wither to dust and life would, for the first time, become an event not worthy of his notice.

Chapter Twenty-One

ဢ

"What is that?" Amanda stared at the article hanging above the bed drowsily. It looked like a spider's web, spun within a circle of branches. Small gems were threaded into the web, and above, where it hung from the ceiling, several small pouches were attached to the string.

"It's a dream catcher." Kiowa lay on his side, snuggled close to her, one arm beneath her head, the other thrown over her stomach as she rested against his chest.

"I've heard of those." She frowned.

Kiowa grunted. "My mother was half Kiowa Indian. She wove it before she sent me away with my grandfather. It's supposed to bring good dreams. To catch visions and hold them in place while allowing nightmares to escape and trouble you no longer."

She tilted her head curiously.

"Most of the Breeds resemble Native Americans, why is that?"

He sighed at her question, shifting onto his back to stare up at the dream catcher.

"The genetically altered sperm has a lot of Native American coding. The scientists, in their studies, decided that it would create fiercer fighters, more savage soldiers when combined with the animal DNA." He shrugged dismissively.

She tilted her head, staring at the intricate, fragile weave and the small crystals that looked like dew upon a spider's web.

"Does it bring good dreams?" she asked him then, turning to look at him.

The expression on his face was a mix of regret and acceptance. He didn't resent the past, but he was determined it wouldn't be repeated.

"It's a keepsake." He finally turned away from it and she knew it was much more than that to him.

She continued to stare up at it silently.

"Did you ever see your mother after your grandfather took you?" she asked. She couldn't imagine her life without her family. As aggravating and frustrating as they could be, they were still her family.

"Never." That unemotional tone again.

She looked over at him as he rose from the bed, seeing the mask firmly in place.

"Are you ready for breakfast yet?"

Amanda eased up in the bed, aware of sore muscles, tender flesh. He had taken her long into the night, riding her with a desperation and a skill that had nearly destroyed them both on several occasions.

"Kiowa," she said softly. "This is why I ran from you last night. If you won't talk to me, then this mating thing is never going to have a chance."

He grunted at that. "Last I heard from you, you weren't giving it a chance anyway." He moved to the dresser and pulled out a change of clothes. "I'm going to get a shower. I'll fix breakfast while you take yours."

Amanda lowered her head, biting her lip nervously.

"I'll keep running, Kiowa."

He stopped. She raised her head, watching the play of muscles beneath his dark skin.

"You run again and I'll make you wish you hadn't." The tone of his voice was frightening, his eyes, when he turned to look at her, were so dead, so dull of emotion that she wondered where he hid the pain and anger she knew must be swirling within him. "Don't make that mistake again, Amanda. For both our sakes."

"The woman that bore you sent that dream catcher." His grandfather pointed to the web, dripping with crystals and feathers that hung from the corner of the living room wall. "She made me promise I'd keep it here with you. Animals don't have dreams though, do they, boy?" he snapped angrily. "It takes a soul to dream."

Kiowa lowered his head, staring down at his hands. He had dreams, soft gentle dreams of a mother singing lullabies, her voice whispering around him.

"Be a good boy, Kiowa. Find your soul..."

His soul. "What was a soul?" the child he had been had questioned daily. It seemed to him that if one had a soul, they wouldn't leave a child alone. They wouldn't leave a child cold, shivering in a shack alone, uncaring of the fears that kept it from sleep.

Did mothers have a soul? he had wondered. How could they have and give their child into the care of such a man?

"You were created, Kiowa," his grandfather had snarled. "Created and forced on a helpless woman. Evil created you and the evil they put in you will destroy you. I should have drowned you like an unwanted pup when you were born."

Kiowa stood beneath the pounding spray of the shower and sighed wearily. The memories were brutal and ones he wished he could banish forever. He should have known better than to leave the life he had created for himself and taken a job that would give him time to reflect.

Amanda made him think of all the soft, gentle things he had once dreamed would be his. At fourteen, leaving the mountain, he had sworn that he would one day have everything his grandfather had made certain he had done without. Instead, Kiowa had learned that the dreams, the magic lives he had seen on the television, were all an illusion. And through the years, he hadn't let himself forget it.

Until Amanda.

Soft, gentle Amanda.

Her laughter had stolen his heart before he had ever touched her. The magic of her smile and the gentleness of her voice had soothed a part of him that he hadn't known still ached. She had made him dream and damn if that didn't hurt.

His lips quirked in wry mockery as he jerked the washrag from the small rack he had placed it on and soaped it quickly.

The mating was a biological, hormonal reaction. It wasn't emotional. It wouldn't miraculously make a woman love what she couldn't accept. Just as motherhood didn't.

"They told her the abomination they were placing in her body," his grandfather raged at him when Kiowa had dared to suggest he *was a child, not an animal. "They showed her the creatures they had whelped so far, mewling, disgusting little animals that looked like a babe and sounded like an animal. You're no more than they were. Forced on her. She birthed you because her conscience wouldn't allow her to do otherwise. But you sickened her from the day you were born..."*

Kiowa flinched at that memory before scrubbing his face roughly with the soapy rag. It was over, but it still had the power to make him bleed. Amanda saw him as an animal, forced upon her by the mating heat, too hard, too rough for the dreams she had. She wanted more than she thought he could give her, and at the end of the day, Kiowa always prided himself on his honesty, if nothing else. There was very little he could give her.

He had enough money from the less than legitimate work he had done over the years, so she wouldn't miss the material things she was used to, because he could provide them. But she was still President Vernon Marion's daughter. Raised to marry an acceptable, elite member of society and to know she was not meant for the dregs of humanity. Kiowa was the dregs of humanity. Hell, some days, he wondered if there was even any humanity left within him.

Long minutes later, freshly showered and dressed in jeans and black t-shirt, he left the bathroom and stared at Amanda as she sat silently in the middle of the bed. She stared back at him with chilly silence, her hazel eyes resentful.

"I'll fix breakfast. You have half an hour," he informed her quietly, pushing the dark needs and his own anger deep into the place he had created for them years ago.

"You have half an hour to think then." She rose from the bed, staring back at him with haughty distain. "You can discuss this, and come to a reasonable solution, or you can start making plans on how best to lock me up. Because this is not going to continue."

"I hope ham and eggs work for you," he said calmly. "I'll have to go down to the storehouse later."

Her lips thinned furiously. "Fix whatever the hell you like. You'll be eating it alone. And think about this, Kiowa. The vote on Breed Law comes up day after tomorrow. How long do you think you can force me to stay here after that?"

She swept past him, her head held high, her hair swirling around her like a short earthen cape as she stomped to the bathroom.

"Never thought I could keep you to begin with," he murmured, quietly. "But that doesn't keep a fool from trying."

Chapter Twenty-Two

ℰ

He was placing the eggs and ham on plates when she walked from the bedroom. Her long hair was still damp, her face pale as she flicked a glance at him.

"Call Dr. Grace back up here," she stated her demand clearly, her voice snapping with authority. "I want those blood tests now."

The arousal was feeding through her body; he could smell it, hotter, brighter than ever before and she was snapping orders at him like a general in the middle of a war zone. Unfortunately for her, Kiowa hadn't joined the Armed Forces simply because he wasn't enamored of orders.

"Eat your breakfast," he growled instead. "Then we'll see if we can't do something to improve your mood."

The smell of her heat was making his mouth water to taste it, to feel it consuming him.

Her head raised slowly, her eyes glittering with fury, with lust when she straightened her shoulders and said, "Over my dead body. I refuse to fuck you again until I've finished those tests."

He frowned at that. He knew how painful the arousal could become. Could she really keep the stubbornness intact that long?

He smiled slowly, remembering the first time, how she had pleaded so sweetly, so heatedly.

"No."

Strangely, a look of hurt passed across her face, as though he had wounded her with that one word.

"I'm not hungry," she said then and turned for the door, swinging it open forcibly before stalking out to the porch, and God only knew how much further.

He stared at the opened door in shock. She was in heat, clearly as aroused as she ever had been, and she was walking away from him? He shook his head before following more slowly, curious as to what she thought she was going to do, or where she was going to go.

Two wolves guarded the porch. Amanda stood at the steps, staring down at the animals that watched her with challenging canine expressions. When she glanced back at him, Kiowa nearly winced at the fury reflecting in her eyes.

"Amanda..." He shoved his hands in the pockets of his jeans and hunched his shoulders defensively. "I cannot stand the thought of the pain you'll be in. Even for the blood tests alone."

"It is not your choice," she snapped, turning away from him and staring down at the wolves. "Tell them to move."

He breathed in roughly. The woman was going to rip his heart from his chest and she didn't even see it. Had no concept of the hell she was forcing him to face.

"It's my place to protect you," he said softly. "How can I do that if I let you do something that will so clearly cause you such pain?" He shook his head in confusion, fighting the impulses to do as she wished and the instinctive howl of the animal that demanded she know no pain.

"Do you think this arousal doesn't hurt?" She turned on him then and the scent of her need had lust ripping through his loins. "High and mighty Coyote Kiowa really doesn't give a fuck though, does he?" she snarled. "If you don't get that scientist back up here, for those tests, then you can watch me hurt anyway, Kiowa. And hurt and hurt. Because you will not touch me until I do this."

"Why is this so important?" He fought the flames of his own anger, the emotion fighting to be free. "They can't help you, Amanda. Nothing can break that bond with me no matter how much you wish it."

"It could create a cure. If nothing else, something that will ease the symptoms," she argued back. "If not for me, then for someone else."

"There is no cure needed." He wanted to bare his teeth in a primal snarl of rage and only barely managed to contain it. "Why are you so desperate to leave me? Isn't it enough for me to know you don't want me?"

She gave him a look of incredulity. "You think this is just about you? That I don't want you? Wouldn't want you even if weren't for this heat?" Her lips thinned, her eyes glittering with unshed tears. "Kiowa, I want to know that what I feel, that what I see in you, is more than just a biological urge gone haywire. And if I can't have it for myself then at least my children will. Now tell those animals to move." Her voice hardened.

The finger that poked into his chest surprised him, stilling the anger long enough for a germ of amusement to enter. She stood before him like an enraged coyote female, her eyes glittering, her teeth bared in her anger and that little finger braced in his chest.

"What about me? What about the rest of the women who endure this? What if something happened to you, moron?" Her voice rose then, and he saw something akin to fear in her eyes. "What do I do then, Kiowa? How much pain will I endure then?"

"Nothing will happen to me." He wouldn't allow it. Not now.

"God, you are so arrogant." She brought her hands to her head, holding it as though in pain. "Forget it. Just forget plain reason. Read my lips instead. I am not fucking you until I have those tests done."

"I'll kill the bastard who hurts you," he yelled back, consumed by his anger now. "Do you hear me, Amanda? I don't care, be it male or female, I will not be able to control my fury."

He was nose to nose with her, forcing himself to hold his hands back to keep from shaking her to make her understand.

"Get over it!" she snapped. "Now get them back up here and then walk away. Go hunting. Hell, go get drunk, I don't give a damn. But if they aren't up here in fifteen minutes flat, then those mangy wolves can bite my ass or clear out, because I'm going to that lab and I'll get the damned things myself."

Son of a bitch. Dammit. Fuck. His dick was throbbing like a toothache, his instincts were screaming at him to fuck her into silence, but something else was warning him that he wasn't going to win this fight. It was what he saw in her eyes. It was one of the very things that had drawn him to her to begin with, that spark of determination, of strength.

She had run from him because of his need to protect her, and now she was in his face, snarling back at him, willing to risk even his rage, which she had no idea what it would entail, to do what she felt was right. To do something that could give her the escape from him that he knew she was looking for.

He moved back slowly, stilling the pain inside him as he looked down at the wolves.

"Go." The single order released them from duty and sent them loping back to Dash, wherever he might be. Then he turned to her. "The labs are in the main house," he said softly. "I can't go with you, Amanda. As much as you may not believe me, I would kill one of those doctors the first time I heard you cry out."

He turned and stalked back into the house. The eggs and ham were left on the table as he paced into the bedroom, drawing in her scent, the presence he feared losing in his life. And he forced himself to wait.

* * * * *

He didn't understand. Amanda swiped at the tears that fell down her face as she stalked down the graveled road. He was so stubborn, so supremely male that she couldn't find the words to explain it.

She was falling in love with him. Stupid fool that she was, in less than a few days, her heart was reaching out to him, her soul yearning for him. And it wasn't just the heat, though that was strong enough to drive even a determined woman insane. No, it went deeper, far too deep for Amanda to ignore the consequences of what they were facing.

As he had said, if word got out of the mating heat, the uncontrollable hunger, the need that burned through even the strongest defenses, then the Breeds would never be safe. To protect her life and the man she was falling in love with, answers would have to be found. And now was the time to find them. Now, when the heat burned inside her like a living brand, and left her shaking, weak from the hunger for his touch.

How she had left him alone at the cabin, she wasn't certain. Hell, she didn't even know if she was going to make it to the estate house at the bottom of the hill her legs were so weak. Everything inside her was screaming at her to go back to him, to touch him, take him inside her.

She couldn't stop crying either. She felt as though it were ripping her soul out to walk away from him like this. To leave him alone, seeing the pain inside him and not knowing how to ease it. Getting him to talk to her was like pulling teeth. Not that talking was so easy when lust ripped at her loins like a hungry beast.

Soon, she promised herself, as soon as these tests were endured and the heat eased, they would talk. If this was nature's way of pairing the Breeds with one particular woman, then Amanda had to trust that nature had paired her as well, with a man who would love her with the same strength and desperation that she was beginning to feel for him.

"Amanda."

She came to a stop as she realized a small utility vehicle had driven up beside her. Looking up, she met Merinus's concerned gaze.

"Kiowa called down to the house. Do you need a ride?"

"He called?" Confusion filled her, but she knew how easy it was to become confused when the desire was climbing to such heights.

"Come on, Amanda, get in. I'll take you back to Kiowa if you like." Her voice was somber, quiet.

Amanda forced herself into the small vehicle.

"No." She shook her head, forcing herself to think, to finish what she had begun. "The tests. We have to do those tests."

"Are you sure? Amanda, you don't have to do this."

But she did. This was her life. Possibly her children's lives. She did have to do this.

"Yes. Yes I do," she whispered, raising her eyes back to Merinus's. "For myself and for Kiowa, I have to do this."

Chapter Twenty-Three
ഇ

"*...As I wish for you dreams that will soothe your soul, dreams that will whisper of secrets untold. I wish for you dreams that will capture you life, dreams so spectacular and bright you can know no strife. I wish for you my child, a dream as brilliant as sunrise, and warm as its gentle rays. But most of all precious one, I dream for you, of many peaceful days.*

"*Sleep now here against me, this moment before our parting. And know I send with you the spirits of the eagle, the wolf and the coyote. To protect you from harm. To raise you in their arms. For mine, sweet precious one, will bring you nothing but harm...*" The voice of past dreams, a young woman, small and wan, her dark eyes filled with misery.

"*They forced you on her...*" A grandfather's hatred.

"*We found the records, Kiowa...*" Dash's words, the day after *Kiowa arrived at the Feline Compound with Amanda.* "*Gina Maria Bear was the daughter of Joseph Mulligan. Kidnapped, held one week, artificially inseminated before she was raped by her guard. A Coyote Breed. Test showed no pregnancy at release, but later notations mention the suspicion that she may have been after they later learned of the longer life span of the Coyote sperm. It's also suspected that the Coyote who raped her, may have forced a second ovulation by mating her. He killed himself a month after her death...*"

"*They opened her up and they shoved you inside her and then they didn't give a damn what happened to her...*" His grandfather's voice had been cruel, filled with hatred. "*She suffered until the day she died, you soulless little bastard...*"

"...Dream of me, Kiowa... Remember me..." The soft voice, was it his mother's? It had haunted him for years, had come to his dreams when life was its bleakest. When a child had struggled to accept the shame and the horror of what his presence had wrought to the unknown mother.

Kiowa stared up at the dream catcher. He had been unable to dispose of it over the years. As it became worn, he had carefully repaired it, kept the wood oiled and supple, the feathers replaced as they became brittle and old. Why?

The image of his dream mother as he once thought of her, drifted through his mind again. Had the guard who raped her, mated her, known what he had done? Had his mother somehow believed her child was safer hidden away from her, in the arms of the grandfather she thought would care for it?

He sighed wearily, dragging himself from the bed, the memories, and the scent of the woman who now tormented him. How was he to know that love could happen like this? That it could rip and shred the soul, tear apart a heart that had shielded itself for more years than he wanted to count.

Nature's curse, the Felines called the mating heat. Was it a curse? Or was it nature's way of ensuring life, of pairing those two souls meant to come together? One half of the other. And who was he to be even considering something so miraculous as a soul mate for himself?

He wandered out of the house and then came stock-still as he faced little Cassie Sinclair just outside the door.

She looked around him then, her blue-gray eyes solemn and curious.

"Amanda is down at the big house, Cassie," he told her quietly, watching her with a frown as she kept looking behind him.

Finally, the little girl looked up at him, those elfin eyes of hers too quiet, too sad.

Cassie was Dash and Elizabeth's child. The little girl had been hunted for months the year before when a drug lord learned that the little girl had been a product of her mother's artificial insemination by wolf/coyote hybrid sperm. Unaware that the doctor who did the procedure hadn't used her husband's sperm, Elizabeth had been unable to fathom why the drug lord was hunting her daughter with such dedication. Somehow Cassie had managed to save them both though when she struck up a pen pal relationship with Dash Sinclair while he was fighting overseas, during one of her few school terms. Dash had come running the minute the little girl's letter for help reached him.

The mating of the Wolf Breed and Elizabeth had produced a healthy son since then, and had created a wave of controversy currently making its rounds in the newspapers.

"I wasn't looking for Amanda," she finally sighed. "My fairy wanted me to come here and meet your fairy."

He blinked down at her in confusion.

"What fairy is that?" Sometimes it was better to just go along with Cassie than to argue with her. She was a strange little girl, always talking to someone no one else could see.

"The fairy that watches you," she said carefully. "I've seen her before, but I'm not allowed to speak to them until I'm spoken to."

Kiowa was beginning to wish she treated real people like that.

"I have a fairy?" His lips twitched at the thought.

"She's very sad," Cassie whispered. "She says you forgot her quilt."

He stilled. Shock resounded through him as he stared back at the child.

"What did you say?" He kept his voice calm, fought the emotion surging within him.

"You forgot the quilt she made you, Kiowa," she said softly. "She whispered her love into each thread and placed powerful protections into its weave. She wanted you to know her mother's love."

He bent down, careful not to move too fast or to make the child feel threatened. She was staring back at him with tear-filled eyes, her hands clenched tightly at her side.

"You see her?" he asked then. "She's here?"

"She says she's always with you," Cassie whispered. "When you allow yourself to dream, she comes through the dream catcher and tries to bring you joy and love. Just as she made certain she brought you to Amanda. But you need to return and get the quilt, Kiowa. She made it just for you."

The quilt. He had left it in the cabin, had never used it when he was there, no matter how cold he got.

"Here, you little bastard. She bought this for you so you wouldn't get cold. I tried to tell her animals don't feel the cold…" He *had thrown the quilt at Kiowa, the hatred in his voice almost maniacal.*

Kiowa had left it lying until he left, then carefully folded it, ignoring the warmth that seemed to reach out to him, and hid it in the metal cupboard in the kitchen. He had left it there when he left the mountain. Not that he had ever forgotten it. But he had wanted nothing to do with the woman who cursed him to the life he led.

"She cries because of what he did," Cassie said then. "Forgive her, Kiowa, she didn't know."

Kiowa clenched his teeth as his chest tightened in pain.

"She always knew you had a soul…"

He came to his feet in a rush, stalking across the porch, away from the little girl.

"Kiowa, don't leave," Cassie called out then. "You've left Amanda alone, and she needs you. But can you help her be strong? Or can you only feed the demons you've known for so long?"

He stopped, turning back to her.

She stood, outlined by the rays of the sun and shadows that made no sense. A chill raced up his back as he realized then what Cassie was. The little girl, created from the altered sperm of both wolf and coyote, holding the traits of each, was psychic. She didn't have fairies; the little girl saw ghosts and they spoke to her.

"Tell her I loved her," he said hoarsely then, thinking of the dreams that had come to him as a child and the comfort they brought.

Cassie nodded slowly. "And she always loved you, Kiowa. She asked that you know, she was coming for you. They knew about you, and about her, and she was coming for you when she was taken from this life. She cried for you."

He grimaced, his lips pulling back from his teeth as his head fell back and he fought the grief that ripped a ragged wound into his heart.

"Let yourself dream, Kiowa," Cassie whispered then. "Let her comfort you again."

He turned from her. He had to get the hell away from her and he had to do it now. Before he saw ghosts himself in the shifting shadows that moved around the child and in his own ragged soul.

Chapter Twenty-Four

ഏ

He intended to escape into the forest, to find the time he needed to still the demons that raged inside him. And he would have, if the cell phone at his side hadn't vibrated insistently.

Snarling, her jerked it off his belt and flipped it open.

"What?"

"Get to the house, Kiowa. Now." Dash's voice was low, imperative.

Kiowa didn't bother answering, he just turned and shot into a dead run down the mountain. Altered genetics and his own athletic awareness gave him the speed and endurance he needed to make it to the main house where Dash waited at the door.

"Listen to me." He pushed Kiowa against the entry wall before he could rush down the hall to the Lab entrance. "She's in pain, Kiowa. And it's bad. But she has to finish this. What's going on right now is too important to stop."

Dash was pale, his blue eyes dark with concern and bleak knowledge.

"What the fuck are you doing to her?" He fought the other man's hold, and would have broken free if both Callan and Kane hadn't lent their strength to holding him still.

"I'll kill all of you," he snarled then.

"And you're welcome to my friend. Later," Dash snapped back. "But right now, you have a mate determined to do what she needs to, and she needs you. We can't hold her, Merinus or Elizabeth can't either. You have to hold her, Kiowa. She can't do this alone."

"You're crazy." He could hear her now. The screams...

"Goddammit, let me go!"

"Kiowa, listen to me. They've found something, inside her." Dash shook him furiously, his own eyes blazing. "She's in full ovulation with the sperm attempting to fertilize. This is important, Kiowa. For God's sake, for all of us, the hormone releasing from her womb now has never been detected before, Kiowa, and in such small amounts that Serena Grace needs the time to collect enough samples of the hormones building in her womb, while Martins follows the ovulation. Listen to me..." Dash was screaming, enraged, his eyes furious, desperate. "For all of us, Kiowa. Your mate is suffering for all of us, help us."

"Kiowa..." He could hear her screaming his name, her voice a lash of agony as it penetrated the careful construction of the Labs.

"Kiowa. For our species. For all of us. If we could do something, anything to make this easier on our mates, then the world will be accepting when they learn of it. We're walking a tightrope between life and hunting season. Help us."

He snarled furiously, throwing his head back against the wall as her cry echoed around him again.

"Let me go to her."

A surge of fury had him tearing from their grasps as he rushed to the opened steel door at the end of the hallway. He hit the stairs at a run, taking them five and six at a time until he vaulted to the steel floor and rushed into the main lab.

It was like a scene from a nightmare.

Amanda was restrained in a gynecological chair, her legs strapped to the stirrups, her arms and hands restrained at the side. Between her spread thighs, Dr. Grace worked slowly as Dr. Martins kept watch on a monitor attached to the camera that was obviously at the mouth of Amanda's womb.

He snarled, drawing their attention, causing Elizabeth and Merinus to rush between him and Dr. Grace.

"Amanda." He moved to her, quickly releasing the straps on her arms as he bent to her. "Hold onto me," he pleaded at her ear as she cried out his name. "Hold onto me, baby. The minute you say the word it stops. I'll make them stop."

She was gasping for breath, her face streaked with tears as her arms wrapped around his shoulders with a desperate grip.

She screamed again, her back trying to bow, the straps across her waist and chest holding her firmly to the chair.

"She's not in any danger." Elizabeth was beside him now. "We're monitoring all her vital signs. The minute her system shows any danger to her, we'll stop."

Kiowa shook his head. He didn't want to hear it.

"The sperm is attempting to fertilize the egg that dropped. There's a small hormonal barrier or shield blocking it. Protecting it from fertilization. But it's weak. Other hormones are releasing into her blood, heightening the arousal. That's what's causing the pain. It's not you touching her..." Elizabeth continued. "It's the mating heat's demand for more sperm, a stronger force to break through the shield. Dr. Grace is attempting to get small quantities of the hormone at a time, to keep from weakening the shield too much to handle the stress against it. It weakens the sperm, Kiowa. Keeps it from getting to the egg. Only a minute amount of that sperm is viable anyway, because of the advanced genetics. That's why the mating heat is demanding intercourse. A greater quantity of sperm to break that barrier. This is a breakthrough we can't ignore. It was a miracle she came to the labs when she did. Dr. Grace detected the change in her blood immediately, just from the studies she's done on mine and Merinus's. This could be what we've waited for..."

Her voice droned on over Amanda's gasps and strangled cries. Amanda was sweating profusely, her skin cold and pale as she shuddered in his grip then tried to arch in agony as a wail echoed around him.

"I love you," he whispered in her ear then, unable to hold the words back, to stem the agony ripping inside his heart. "Let me stop this, Amanda. Let me take you out of here."

"No." She gasped, her nails digging into his shoulders as convulsive tremors shook her body. "Have to. Have to. For both of us, Kiowa."

"We're almost done, Amanda." Dr. Grace's voice was tear-roughened, and Kiowa hated realizing that. "Just a little bit more."

"The viable sperm have nearly exhausted themselves," Dr. Martin reported. "As soon as you're finished, extract the camera. If the rest break through, then it's God's will."

God's will. Nature's curse.

Kiowa clenched his teeth as Amanda screamed out in agony again.

"Kiss me, Kiowa," she cried out then. "Please I hate this. I hate sounding like this. Make me stop."

"Ah God. Baby..." His lips covered hers, his tongue plunging inside her as she met him with a desperation that broke his heart.

Her lips sucked at his tongue and he tasted the release of the hormone, filled her mouth with it and gave her what she needed. He muffled her screams, held her to his chest and did all he could to comfort her when he wanted to do nothing more than kill those hurting her.

"My God..." Dr. Grace's voice was ecstatic. "My God. Dr. Martin, look at that. Do you see the change? It's a new hormone. My God, we're going to crack this."

Kiowa didn't give a damn what they were doing. Amanda was kissing him as though both their lives depended it, and though she still flinched and shuddered with pain, at least those agonized cries had been smothered.

She was sleeping. Finally. Hours later, Kiowa carried Amanda into the cabin, laid her gently in the bed they had shared and pulled the blankets around her. She had finally escaped the pain the only way she could. She had passed out.

Sitting beside her, he smoothed her hair back from her face before leaning down to kiss her lips gently.

He didn't know what the hell had happened in that lab, but both scientists had begun shouting orders back and forth, babbling about additional samples, blood and new hormones. He didn't give a damn. He just wanted her out of there, away from the pain she had deliberately inflicted on herself.

"I'm okay..." Her voice was hoarse as her eyes opened weakly, her lashes fluttering against her cheeks.

"Yeah. You are," he whispered, his hand smoothing over her hair as he gazed down at her bleakly.

What the hell was he going to do without her? If they created a hormonal block, or even a cure for the mating heat, how would he survive losing her?

"I had to do it, Kiowa," she said then, her eyes reflecting her own inner turmoil. He could see the battle waging within her, though he had no idea what it was over.

He breathed in deeply.

"Dash managed to unearth the Council reports on my mother," he said softly, staring down at her, knowing he couldn't hold her forever. "She wasn't just held and artificially inseminated. When it was realized she wouldn't conceive, evidently one of her guards raped her...and mated her." He swallowed tightly. "I never intended to force you into this. I kissed you because you were going to scream. I continued because I couldn't stop. I would do it again."

A weak smile tugged at the corner of her lips.

"No excuses, huh?" she asked then.

"None." He didn't believe in them.

"I wouldn't have missed it for the world, Kiowa," she said, her eyes drooping sleepily. "Now, I do want to go home..." The end of what she would have said slurred slowly until sleep took her.

She fell asleep as she shattered his soul.

He leaned down, kissed her soft lips and breathed in roughly.

"I love you, Mate," he whispered then. "I'll always love you."

Then he stood and walked to the dresser. Ovulation was over, there would be relief for her, at least for a while. Long enough he prayed, for her to forgive him, but he doubted it.

There were few things to pack. He didn't own a lot. His guns, his knives, the tools of his trade. A few changes of clothes, his jacket. He was packed within the hour and standing on the porch steps, once again staring back at Dash Sinclair.

"Did she conceive?" Kiowa asked, his voice controlled. Calm.

"There was no conception." Dash crossed his arms over his chest and glanced at Kiowa's duffel bag. "The additional hormone is looking like a blocker," he reported. "According to preliminary tests, it could be used to ease the effects of the mating heat. It could be years before we're certain though. Dr. Grace doesn't think she retrieved enough to actually make any headway."

Kiowa nodded bleakly.

"Let her know if she needs me...whenever...I'll come to her."

"Why not just stay, Kiowa?" Dash asked him then. "She's your mate. You know you'll never be satisfied without her. And the threat against her may not be over. The blood supremacists somehow managed to blackmail one of the Secret Service agents protecting her. He drugged the others so no one could help her."

"I can't force her." He shook his head. "This wasn't her dream, Dash. It's not my life she wanted. I won't take that from her. But I'll make certain she's protected. I'll always protect her."

He picked up his duffel bag and moved down the steps.

"Kiowa. Your mother didn't remarry," he said then. "The final report came in last night. Your grandfather lied to you. There was no marriage, no other family. From what the investigators found, she spent those years searching for you and her father. I don't believe she willingly gave you up. The investigators say that for a period of a year and a half, both Joseph Mulligan and his daughter disappeared. When she resurfaced, she was searching for her father. I believe he kidnapped you after he learned what happened."

"It doesn't matter now." Kiowa shrugged, careful to keep his expression blank, the pain inside. "It's over now and they're all dead, Dash. Every one of them. Tell Amanda I said goodbye."

He walked away. Each step was a burden; every foot away from the cabin was another knife in his heart. He would come to her, if she needed him. But he wouldn't force anymore from her than he already had. He would let her live her dream, and he would dream of what could have been.

Chapter Twenty-Five
Colorado Mountains

❧

The cabin wasn't as big as he remembered it being. Kiowa stepped into the dim light of the well-made log structure and stared at the small living room with a man's vision rather than a child's hatred.

The television was still mounted to the wall, the collection of movie discs stacked around it. There were dozens of movie discs. His grandfather, Joseph Mulligan, hadn't scrimped in the education he had meant to give Kiowa. Books lined the walls, a layer of dust covering them, the dull, fine powder covered the entire room.

To the side was the bathroom. A tiny cubicle with a bath and toilet. It was dark, heavy with oppressed silence. Next to it was the bedroom Kiowa had never used. He could see the bed from where he stood, the narrow lines unbroken, still perfectly made with the thin sheet that had covered it during the years he had lived there. Alone.

He stepped through the room, heedless of the tracks he made in the dusty floor and entered the kitchen.

A chair sat beneath the small table in a corner. The stove and refrigerator separated by the sink on the other wall. The cupboard sat in the same place it always had been, duller, smaller than he remembered.

He walked to it, opened the squeaking door slowly and stared inside.

The quilt was there, just as perfectly folded as it had been when he placed it on the shelf. A can of beans sat on the bottom shelf. A few magazines on another. It was as empty as his childhood had been. As empty as his life was now. Leaving

Amanda had been the hardest thing he had ever done in his life.

Reaching out, he touched the quilt, feeling the warmth he remembered feeling, even as a child when his grandfather had thrown it at him. So much rage. His grandfather had hated him with a strength that still had the power to cause regret to well within him.

Had his mother been searching for him when she had died? He assumed it was possible. Vaguely, he remembered a time before his grandfather had brought him to the cabin. Joseph had moved him around a lot, always traveling, always slipping in and out of town in the dead of night.

Kiowa's investigation over the years as he searched for any other family had turned up surprising facts about the man. A religious fanatic. He had been a man that Kiowa often thought would have fit in well with the blood supremacists.

He shook his head wearily. It was too late for answers, the mystery of why his mother had given him into Mulligan's care would likely always haunt him. For so many years he had thought she had found happiness, that she had put him and his existence to the back of her mind and that she never bothered to think of the child that had been forced on her.

He reached in and gathered the quilt from the shelf, tucking it under his arm as he turned to leave the room. As he turned, he came to an abrupt stop as he came face to face with Amanda.

It had been nearly two weeks since he had seen her. Nights filled with a cold emptiness that he felt swallowed by. A loneliness he had never known, not even as a child, had eaten at him.

She was dressed as he had often seen her before he was forced to rescue her, mate her. Jeans molded her slender legs and a heavy cream sweater covered her full breasts, the loose material falling just past her hips. Her long beautiful hair flowed around her, thicker, more silken-looking than he remembered.

"Mighty Kiowa," she said quietly as she leaned against the doorframe. "You're a tough man to catch up with."

She was angry. He could smell it on the crisp air that filled the cabin.

"How did you get here?" he asked her rather than answering her comment.

"Dash flew me in when he got word you were sighted in Denver," she answered calmly, though her hands were clenched as she crossed them over her breasts. "He's been looking for you ever since I woke up."

"That doesn't tell me why you're here." He could push past her, continue into the bleak existence he assumed lay outside that cabin door, but he had already walked away from her once, he wasn't strong enough to do it a second time.

Even angry, the scent of her wrapped around his senses, making him hunger for her with a power that still failed to amaze him.

"Daddy wanted to meet you," she finally said. "After the celebration of the passing of Breed Law, he wanted to thank you for rescuing me. He was disappointed."

Kiowa snorted at that. "He didn't know the truth then."

"No. Not all of it," she agreed, breathing in deeply. "Why did you leave like that? Without saying goodbye?"

"I wouldn't have been able to leave if I had said goodbye, Amanda," he finally said starkly. "I did it the best I could. And you shouldn't have followed me like this. It was hard enough to give you back your life. You should have taken it and run."

"Was that what you did?" She arched her brow mockingly then. "Gave me back my life? I was unaware anyone had stolen it from me."

His teeth clenched at the deliberate sarcasm in her voice.

171

"This wasn't the life you wanted, Amanda," he snapped then. "You wanted to go home, back to your own dreams."

"And you couldn't have been a part of that?" Oh yes, she was angry. The scent of it filled the air like a blast of heat. "Is trotting from hellhole to hellhole more important than being with me? To working out a life we could both be satisfied with?"

He stared at her in surprise before shaking his head in confusion.

"You're the President's daughter, Amanda. How easily do you think your world would accept me? A Coyote Breed, one with no last name, no education. How long before you began to see what everyone did and hated me for the life you became trapped within?"

"Oh, poor Kiowa?" She was snarling with her fury. "Aren't you just so full of self-sacrifice? Or is that bullshit you're so full of?"

Surprise surged through him, as did a kernel of amusement.

"I've been accused of both." He shrugged as though unconcerned, though a building hope was surging within him.

"I can understand why." She was flushed, her eyes glittering with anger, her body trembling with it.

"Why are you here, Amanda?" Point-blank, there was no sense in beating around the bush any longer. "I walked away and gave you what you asked for. After the hell you endured to escape me, what else did you expect?"

"To escape you? You think I went through those nightmarish tests so I could escape you, Kiowa?" she asked incredulously, straightening from the doorframe then as she stared back at him in furious amazement. "I did that for us. For any child we conceived. Do you think I want our children enduring what we had to go through? Being thrown into the morass of emotions and needs that half the time makes no sense and the rest of the time are nothing less than infuriating? What I did, I did for us. Not to escape you."

He could only stare back at her, pushing back hope, stilling the welling emotions threatening to consume him.

"You wanted to go home," he reminded her.

"With you," she cried out. "I wanted you to see my life, too. I wanted you to see the joy of a child's laughter, sit with you in the evenings and just be at peace. Show you my house that I worked so hard for and fix you dinner from those stupid cookbooks I bought. I wanted you to see the other side before we decided our next move. I didn't ask you to leave me."

"So you assumed I could read your mind instead?" He growled in frustration. "Dammit it, Amanda, I could have no more known that was what you wanted than I could have known where a bird would shit next."

She blinked at the crude phrasing. "That was uncalled for." Her eyes narrowed warningly. "You expect me to read your mind. To know from one minute to the next what that blank mask you slide into place means. If I can put up with that then you can learn to read my particular mind. It's not that hard, you know," she sneered with feminine contempt.

He wanted to laugh out loud. He wanted to let the grin that filled his soul free, but he held it back, watching as she stared at him with fierce fury.

She was his woman. She hadn't run from it, hadn't hated him when the heat eased.

"You still don't get it do you, Kiowa?" she asked him softly, miserably. "I love you. The heat wasn't just physical. With every touch, every confrontation, you took another piece of my heart. I stopped trying to understand it or to explain it. It's just there. Then you left as though it didn't matter." There was the anger then, fueled by her pain, a pain he couldn't bear to see.

"I couldn't force this on you," he whispered, moving to her, dropping the quilt to the table as he neared her. "I couldn't stay and not have you, Amanda. Not take you with every breath I have. Don't you understand that? I had to let you go."

He stood only inches from her, feeling the warmth of her nearness, smelling not just her anger and her arousal, but something else. Something sweet and clear that seemed to fill the air around her. Love.

"What now?" she asked him solemnly, staring up at him, indecision shadowing her eyes. "I don't want to lose you, Kiowa. I can't lose you."

"You never could." He touched her face gently, his fingertips relishing the touch of her silken skin and the warmth that vibrated from her flesh. "I love you, Amanda. With everything I am. Every part of me. Soul deep, baby, I love you."

It was more than a mating heat, more than a biological or chemical reaction. It was, as Kiowa had thought before leaving her, a pairing of souls. It didn't have to make sense. It didn't have to be pretty or gentle or kind, and he doubted such pairings ever were. It just was.

"Let's get out of here." He picked up the quilt, a part of his past he regretted leaving behind, when he regretted nothing else.

"The dream catcher is in my house now," she told him fiercely. "If you want it back, I guess you'll have to endure living with me for a while. I have to finish the school term. Then we can decide what to do."

He shrugged his powerful shoulders. "I can work anywhere."

"I guess bouncers are in high demand?" She gave him a laughing look as he led her out the door.

"Well." He cleared his throat uncomfortably. "So are independent computer programmers and security analysts. I've been doing that for years. Dash just hasn't accessed the information yet."

He loved knowing something the other man didn't. It gave him a real sense of accomplishment.

"I knew you were a bad boy," she laughed up at him as he pressed a kiss to her forehead and led her from the cabin into the late fall air.

The jeep waited just below the cabin yard. So did the little black stealth helicopter Dash had flown her in on. The other man stood just beside the opened cockpit door a smile flashing across his face as he lifted his hand in farewell. At least for now. Kiowa was under no illusions that the other man wouldn't try to connive him into helping him again whenever the need arose. Dash Sinclair was determined to find a place in society for the Breeds, and for his own small family.

The helicopter lifted into the air on a near silent swirl of wind as Kiowa helped Amanda into the jeep. Closing her door he moved quickly to his own, jumping in and cranking the engine before turning to look at her.

"I think you need to be spanked," he drawled then. "I'm sure you did something naughty after I left."

Her face flushed, her eyes glowing then with lust and love and a pleasure he felt clear to the bottom of his feet.

"Oh, I'm sure I was very naughty," she agreed with a wicked little smile. "You might even have to tie me down and torture me a little bit. Teach me a lesson so to speak."

His cock, already painfully engorged jerked in his jeans.

He smiled, displaying the longer, curved canines at the side of his mouth.

"I'm going to bite you again," he promised her then. He ached to feel her beneath him, shuddering as he held her in place with his mouth at her neck, his cock swelling inside her.

She glanced at him then from beneath her lashes and licked her lips slowly.

"If I let you."

Anticipation coiled hot and heavy in his loins then. If she let him.

He reversed the jeep and turned quickly, heading down the steep track toward town and the closest damned motel he could check into. He would see just how much she would let him do then. Or more to the point, just how much he could convince her to let him do.

Chapter Twenty-Six

❧

The hotel room was dim, the fading light of day barely penetrating the thick curtains as Amanda preceded Kiowa into the room. The bed looked huge. She couldn't look anywhere else as a sudden case of nerves began to flutter in the pit of her stomach.

What if she had been wrong? What if it was the mating heat alone that had drawn them together, made the sex so desperate and filled with pleasure?

She stood silently in the center of the room, fighting to calm the sudden fear that rose inside her. When she awoke to learn he had left, rage and grief had swelled within her in a wave that had nearly destroyed her. Surely, that was love?

"Take your clothes off."

She shivered at his hard voice, so dark and wicked, so husky it seemed to vibrate from the very depths of his chest. It was rough and guttural and she couldn't halt the little shudder of pleasure that raced over her body.

She licked her lips and glanced up at him as he moved around her, walking slowly to the bed and sitting down.

"I'm sure you were a very naughty girl while I was away," he said reprovingly. "You know I'll have to punish you."

Oh God. It was her hottest fantasy come to life. The dimness of the room made him seem darker, stronger somehow, as though that were possible.

"What if I promise to be good now?" She played into her own sexual fantasy, her pussy weeping at the thrill that shot through her.

He chuckled at that. "I'm sure you will be. After tonight. Now take off your clothes. You don't want me to have to cut them off."

She barely restrained her moan. Oh yes she did.

"Start with the shoes. Take everything off very slowly."

She could barely breathe; her knees were shaking, her hands trembling with excitement.

She kicked her shoes off. That part was easy. Her hands lifted to the buttons of her blouse, and there her battle began. She could feel her swollen breasts, the tight hot nipples that peaked them, rubbing against the lace of her bra and she wanted to cry out just at that small pleasure.

She struggled with the tiny buttons, her fingers slipping, becoming uncooperative as he continued to watch her with his hot black eyes. Her gaze flickered up, her breath catching as he rose to his feet.

"Are you trying to tease me?" he asked her, as wicked, wicked sensuality echoed in his voice.

"No." She shook her head fiercely as he circled her. "I'm not."

His hand cupped the curve of her butt.

"I think you are. I think you know how hard my cock is, how eager my tongue is to taste you and you're teasing me."

Her breath caught in her throat. Yeah, that was it.

"No. I promise. I'm trying to be good," she whispered breathlessly.

This was just too exciting. It was everything she had ever fantasized about and more.

A second later a moan rippled from her throat as his hand landed firmly on the curve of her ass. The stinging little fire shot straight to her pussy and had it flooding with hot, rich cream.

"You'll have to pay for this," he whispered at her ear then. "Put your hands behind your back, Amanda."

Oh God. Oh God.

She had seen the length of rope he had collected from the Jeep and stuck in his jeans pocket before they entered the hotel. She moved slowly, trembling in anticipation as she crossed her wrists at the small of her back.

"I'm going to enjoy this, Amanda," he breathed at her ear. "Are you?"

She was going to come before he ever touched her at this rate.

Amanda was panting by time he bound her wrists firmly behind her back, the rope holding her fast as she tugged at the knot.

"Now, how are we going to get these clothes off you?" he murmured as he brushed her hair back from her neck, his breath whispering across the wound he had made there the first time he had taken her.

She shuddered again, her breath catching in her throat as his tongue licked over the wound, his hands smoothing up her stomach until he was cupping the heaving mounds of her breasts.

"Any suggestions?" he asked her, his thumb and forefinger gripping her nipples and tweaking them firmly.

She shook her head fiercely. She hoped he didn't truly expect her to talk. She could barely breathe, let alone form actual words.

"Oh God!" Okay, she could talk.

The sound of fabric ripping tore through the room as he jerked the blouse free of the delicate buttons anchoring it. It hung on her then, barely clinging to the rapid rise and fall of her swollen breasts as his hands dragged it over her shoulders, his teeth scraping at the mating mark on her neck.

She was going to come. Right then and there, standing in the middle of the room she was going to climax to nothing else but the excitement tearing through her. Then he walked away from her. She stared at his back as he disappeared into the bathroom, listened to the sound of running water, and seconds later watched as he sauntered back.

He was watching her with dark, lust-filled eyes, but there was no sign, no reason why, he had disappeared in such a way. Then it didn't matter, because he was standing in front of her, his hands cupping her breasts, lifting them in the lace cups of her bra and breathing softly across her nipples before his teeth nipped at them.

"I'm going to make you scream for me," he whispered as he rubbed his cheeks between the mounds.

That sounded damned good to her.

"But first, I have to get you out of those clothes, don't I?"

The scrape of steel through leather had her eyes opening wide as he pulled the hunting knife from the sheath at his side. The hilt glistened damply in the low light, the rounded tip drawing her gaze as a weak moan filtered from her lips.

The blade slid beneath the middle of her bra, cutting through the fabric with a soft hiss. The straps were given the same treatment, each severed thread revealing more until the scraps fell away from her body and Amanda was certain she was going to collapse into a puddle of weak desire at his feet.

"Very pretty," he whispered, lifting his other hand and weighing a swollen mound within his palm. "Such hard, sweet little nipples. Do you want me to taste your nipples Amanda?"

"God yes." She was panting, fighting for breath as she forced the words past her lips.

Heat was moving through her body, searing her nerve endings and setting fire to every cell she possessed.

He bent closer, his tongue licking over one distended peak as she shuddered helplessly.

"Please... Please... Please..." She was begging, willing to cry, whatever it took to get what she needed.

"Naughty girl," he whispered against her nipple a second before his tongue curled around it again, drawing it into his mouth where his teeth enclosed it firmly.

Her pussy convulsed, spilling her juices between her legs to soak the silk panties she wore beneath her jeans. She clenched her thighs, gasping at the pleasure tearing through her body.

He chuckled then, withdrawing and stepping behind her. Within minutes he had cut every shred of clothing from her body. Kneeling behind her, he pulled the ruined pieces of cloth away from her, then kissed the cheek of her rear before scraping his teeth over it firmly.

"Kiowa," she moaned roughly, her knees trembling as she fought to stay on her feet.

He was running the hilt of that knife up and down her thigh, the cool leather rasping across her flesh as his tongue flickered over the narrow valley between the cheeks of her ass.

"Bad girls get punished," he whispered as his tongue tautened and pressed between the cheeks he was tormenting, leaving a path of fire in its wake as the hilt of the knife slid higher on her thigh. "It's time to begin your punishment, Amanda."

Oh God yes. Finally. Finally.

The soft leather slid further along her thigh as his arm wrapped around her hips. Holding her in place.

"Spread your thighs." He was breathing hard now, the heated whisper of his breath caressing her buttocks.

She shifted, spreading her legs wider, moaning as the handle slid through thick hot cream just a little higher. It rubbed against her swollen pussy lips, sent pleasure shooting into her clit.

Then it was parting the soft folds, coming close and closer...

"Damn you!" she cursed roughly when it was abruptly removed.

181

"Did I say you could speak?" Harsh, guttural, his voice snapped out as his hand landed on her butt. The small, tingling slap had her pressing back against him, her hands twisting behind her desperately as more of her juices flowed from her pussy.

Then he was pressing the hilt against her again, sliding it through the narrow slit until it butted against the entrance to her vagina.

"Beg for it," he ordered her harshly. "Beg me to fuck you, Amanda."

"Fuck me," she gasped, knowing that only the arm that had returned around her hips was holding her upright. "Please, Kiowa, please fuck me."

It penetrated. The soft leather parted her flesh, slid in her slick juices and began to stretch her erotically. It was the most decadent thing she had ever heard of. She hadn't read anything so decadent.

The hilt of the knife parted her, sliding slowly, deeply inside her as a wail of pleasure shattered the silence of the room. Then it was sliding free, no matter how she pleaded, how she begged for more, it was removed as he stood slowly behind her.

"You aren't allowed to come yet," he whispered at her ear before moving in front of her. "Bad girls have to wait to come, Amanda."

"I'll be good," she cried desperately. "I promise, Kiowa. I'll be so good."

"Will you?" He removed his shirt quickly as he kicked his moccasins free. "Let's see how good you can be."

His pants were removed slowly, the thick, engorged length of his cock revealed as he tossed the material aside.

"On your knees, Amanda. Show me what a good girl you can be."

She went to her knees, staring up at the wide head of his cock as it came toward her. Her mouth watered as hunger pierced the core of her womb, proving her arousal, her need for this man wasn't just a product of mating heat but a product of the love she had held within her soul, waiting for the man who could tap not just her love, but her greatest desires as well.

She opened her lips over the broad crest, moaning in desperate need as she felt the first pulse of the pre-come. Elizabeth had finally explained the lubricating hormone that pulsed from his cock. The fluid eased tight muscles, gave them a flexibility as they blocked pain and allowed the incredible pleasure of the final, climatic swelling of the male's cock.

It only happened with mates. That was why Kiowa had been surprised when it happened that night in the Jeep. He hadn't known it could happen, had no idea that nature had provided him such tools to please a woman.

And please her it did. He tasted of honey and spice, an aphrodisiac all its own as it filled her senses.

She encased the head of his erection in her mouth, her tongue rippling against the sensitive underside as his fingers slid into her hair. She watched his taut abdomen flex, tighten as a growl vibrated from his throat.

Amanda moaned at the sound, her lips tightening around his surging cock as he began to thrust slow and easy between her lips. She licked and suckled hungrily at the thick flesh, feeling the ridged veins throb with the flow of blood as they passed over her tongue and sensitive lips.

"Fuck. That's good." His voice was a tormented groan. "Suck it deep, baby. That's a good girl. You can be a good girl can't you, baby?"

She moaned in reply, taking him deeper as he began to move more firmly in and out of her mouth, fucking her in short, hard strokes that made her pussy weep in hunger. She was moaning around his cock, sucking at it hungrily, her hands clenching into fists with her need to touch him.

His hands were in her hair, his fingers clenching the thick strands as he tugged at them, creating an arousing, fiery friction that left her crying out with the sensation. God it was so good, too good. She was only a breath away from climax and she knew it.

"Damn your mouth is hot." His words sent a spear of aching need straight to her womb. "And your tongue is so soft, so sweet on my dick. Suck it, baby. Just a little bit harder..."

She sucked harder, her tongue lashing at it, feeling the ripples of impending release that throbbed beneath her tongue a second before he pulled free.

"No." She tried to follow him, to draw him back, only to have him sit down hard on the bed and pull her quickly over his thighs.

There was no time to cry out before his hand landed on her upraised ass. She could only twist in his grip, desperate to get closer, feeling her clit swell and throb with each swat to her delicate flesh.

Fire bloomed along the cheeks of her ass, sizzled across nerve endings and sent darts of pleasure so extreme she could barely stand it, straight to her pussy. She was so wet the juices were dampening the insides of her thighs, her cunt dripping in hungry demand before he lifted her and tossed her to the bed.

"Raise your ass...higher." He moved behind her as she struggled to her knees, her bound hands making it difficult to get in the proper position.

A second later the rope was sliding free of her hands before he gripped her hips, pulled them into position and tucked the head of his cock at the entrance to her weeping cunt.

The first blast of pre-come had a strangled scream erupting from her throat as she tried to back closer, to force him inside her. He waited a second, pressed closer and another jetting eruption of the fluid filled her pussy.

"Now, baby, this is how bad girls get fucked... Hard and deep..." He pushed inside in one heavy thrust that sent the thick flesh pushing past tight, well-lubricated muscles and burying him to the hilt in soft willing flesh.

She screamed then. An inarticulate sound of pleasure and pain and a need for more that threatened to shatter her mind. It was so good. So damned good it was going to kill her.

"Do you like that, Amanda?" He pulled free only to surge inside her again, sending her senses spinning, her body burning as her back arched and she lunged into the thrust.

"Oh, you do like that." His hand landed heavily on her upraised ass. "Only bad girls like that, Amanda. You said you were a good girl."

"I'm bad," she cried desperately. "Oh God, Kiowa, I'm such a bad girl. Do it again. Please do it again." She was not above begging when the situation warranted it. And right now, oh baby, was it warranted.

He paddled her rear again as he began to drive into her, fast hard strokes that kept her just a breath from climax, as his free hand held her hips in place and kept her from following him, from increasing the force of the thrust.

"Tell me to bite you, Amanda," he suddenly groaned, and she knew he was close to the end of his own control. "God please, baby, let me bite you."

"Bite me!" She was screaming the words as she felt his thrusts increase, felt his cock ramming into her, sliding heatedly through his own pre-come and the thick cream that coated her.

Her orgasm was getting closer. So close. Just another breath, another thrust.

He came over her, as he pulled her hair out of the way, a growl, animalistic and rough sounding at her ear a second before his teeth bit into her shoulder, his tongue rasping the wound and sending her over the edge.

She lost reality. Hell, reality nothing, she lost her mind as the pleasure-pain of the bite and his hard driving thrusts pushed her over the edge and she exploded into a cataclysm of bursting lights and sensation. Every nerve ending detonated in pleasure. Every cell swelled in rapture until the release poured from her, only to be stopped by the fist-hard swelling that locked her mate deep inside her cunt as his seed began to pulse from his cock to fill her hungry womb.

Each hard spurt of semen triggered another smaller explosion in her pussy. Each hard throb of the knot locked inside her had her screaming in pleasure until she could do nothing but lay beneath him, shuddering convulsively, the ecstasy never-ending as he moaned his own pleasure at her neck.

Finally, hours, days later. But it could have just been minutes. She moaned weakly as she felt the swelling decrease and his cock slide regretfully from the hot grip she had on it.

He collapsed beside her, pulling her into his arms, surrounding her with his warmth as exhaustion began to slip over her.

"I love you, Kiowa," she whispered against his damp chest as she felt sleep steal over her. "Forever."

He kissed her brow gently. "Soul deep, Amanda. I love you. Soul deep."

Epilogue

ℬ

The wedding of Amanda Marion, daughter to President Vernon Marion and Coyote Breed Kiowa Bear was performed at the Feline Breed compound in Virginia late Saturday afternoon with over 1000 guests in attendance.

The Feline Breed compound, now named Sanctuary, opened its doors for the first time for more than just the wounded and weary Breeds rescued from various Labs around the world. Dignitaries, politicians and royalty alike attended the event, which this reporter was privileged to see as well.

The bride wore a traditional, long white gown and veil, as the groom, dressed entirely in black, watched her approach with nothing less than adoration. It has been this reporter's pleasure to attend each ceremony so far performed among the Breeds. The wedding of Callan Lyons and Merinus. Taber Reynolds and his wife Roni, Kane Tyler and his wife, Sherra and now, Kiowa Bear and his petite wife, Amanda.

For the time being, the happy couple will return to her Pennsylvania home where Mrs. Bear will continue teaching and Mr. Bear will set up his computer analysis and programming business within their home.

President Marion was all smiles during and after the ceremony, where he toasted the happy couple and then kissed his daughter fondly before she entered the helicopter that would whisk her and her new husband to an undisclosed honeymoon location.

With the passing of Breed Law, and new Breeds arriving daily within the compound, the blood supremacists are becoming even more outspoken in regards to this new species of human. Thurman Truman, president of the Society of Untainted Genetics, announced yesterday that he will further his efforts to find the proof necessary to convince the world that the Breeds are indeed an inferior species and

187

because of their animal genetics should be classed as subhuman, rather than being given the classification of Human, as the Senate decided weeks before.

The radical groups are becoming more vocal, and in many ways, alienating the very people they are trying to convince to join their ranks as their hysteria-induced speeches rage along the airwaves. The Feline Breed compound, Sanctuary, is now doubling its security and with the additional land the government has added to it, making plans to be assured of their own protection even as many law enforcement groups around the nation are making efforts to use the special abilities of the Breeds within their own ranks.

A special taskforce of Breed and military personnel is now being formed under a special section of the Law Enforcement Act of 2020, which gives police, DEA and the FBI special license to use extreme measures in preserving the defense and safety of the nation. This special taskforce will be tested against the most difficult assignments facing these agencies.

President Marion's goal is to see that the Breeds are, within his four year term, given every access to the same freedoms and rights the citizens of this great country have enjoyed for centuries, while the blood supremacists are working to undermine the very foundations now being put in place.

Research into the history of our great land shows the price and the horrors of prejudice. For as long as time has been measured and history recorded, such mistakes have been shown to cost society and its people an exacting price in following such principles. We built this land and preserved our democracy against all threats, great and small, and against all prejudices that have come our way. We have, at points in time, made a mockery of human kindness and at other times, have shown a mercy as enduring as life itself.

This reporter, in watching the historic events of this new species of human unfold, can only wonder at the choices we will now make, in a time when historians and psychologists alike state that civilization is at its peak of human awareness. Will we accept, or will we once again sink into the mistakes of the past? Only time can tell…

Also by Lora Leigh

❧

A Wish, A Kiss, A Dream (*anthology*)
B.O.B.'s Fall (*with Veronica Chadwick*)
Bound Hearts 1: Surrender
Bound Hearts 2: Submission
Bound Hearts 3: Seduction
Bound Hearts 4: Wicked Intent
Bound Hearts 5: Sacrifice
Bound Hearts 6: Embraced
Bound Hearts 7: Shameless
Cowboy & the Captive
Dragon Prime
Elemental Desires (*anthology*)
Ellora's Cavemen: Tales from the Temple I (*anthology*)
Feline Breeds 1: Tempting the Beast
Feline Breeds 2: The Man Within
Feline Breeds 3: Kiss of Heat
Law and Disorder: Moving Violations (*with Veronica Chadwick*)
Legacies 1: Shattered Legacy
Legacies 2: Shadowed Legacy
Legacies 3: Savage Legacy
Manaconda (*anthology*)
Men of August 1: Marly's Choice
Men of August 2: Sarah's Seduction
Men of August 3: Heather's Gift
Men of August 4: August Heat
Sealed With a Wish
Wizard Twins 1: Menage A Magick
Wizard Twins 2: When Wizards Rule
Wolf Breeds 1: Wolfe's Hope
Wolf Breeds 2: Jacob's Faith
Wolf Breeds 3: Aiden's Charity

Wolf Breeds 4: Elizabeth's Wolf

About the Author

ॐ

Lora Leigh is a wife and mother living in Kentucky. She dreams in bright, vivid images of the characters intent on taking over her writing life, and fights a constant battle to put them on the hard drive of her computer before they can disappear as fast as they appeared.

Lora's family, and her writing life co-exist, if not in harmony, in relative peace with each other. An understanding husband is the key to late nights with difficult scenes, and stubborn characters. His insights into human nature, and the workings of the male psyche provide her hours of laughter, and innumerable romantic ideas that she works tirelessly to put into effect.

Lora welcomes comments from readers. You can find her website and email address on her author bio page at www.ellorascave.com.

Tell Us What You Think

We appreciate hearing reader opinions about our books. You can email us at Comments@EllorasCave.com.

Why an electronic book?

We live in the Information Age—an exciting time in the history of human civilization, in which technology rules supreme and continues to progress in leaps and bounds every minute of every day. For a multitude of reasons, more and more avid literary fans are opting to purchase e-books instead of paper books. The question from those not yet initiated into the world of electronic reading is simply: *Why?*

1. *Price.* An electronic title at Ellora's Cave Publishing and Cerridwen Press runs anywhere from 40% to 75% less than the cover price of the exact same title in paperback format. Why? Basic mathematics and cost. It is less expensive to publish an e-book (no paper and printing, no warehousing and shipping) than it is to publish a paperback, so the savings are passed along to the consumer.

2. *Space.* Running out of room in your house for your books? That is one worry you will never have with electronic books. For a low one-time cost, you can purchase a handheld device specifically designed for e-reading. Many e-readers have large, convenient screens for viewing. Better yet, hundreds of titles can be stored within your new library—on a single microchip. There are a variety of e-readers from different manufacturers. You can also read e-books on your PC or laptop computer. (Please note that Ellora's Cave does not endorse any specific brands.

You can check our websites at www.ellorascave.com or www.cerridwenpress.com for information we make available to new consumers.)

3. *Mobility.* Because your new e-library consists of only a microchip within a small, easily transportable e-reader, your entire cache of books can be taken with you wherever you go.

4. *Personal Viewing Preferences.* Are the words you are currently reading too small? Too large? Too… ANNOYING? Paperback books cannot be modified according to personal preferences, but e-books can.

5. *Instant Gratification.* Is it the middle of the night and all the bookstores near you are closed? Are you tired of waiting days, sometimes weeks, for bookstores to ship the novels you bought? Ellora's Cave Publishing sells instantaneous downloads twenty-four hours a day, seven days a week, every day of the year. Our webstore is never closed. Our e-book delivery system is 100% automated, meaning your order is filled as soon as you pay for it.

Those are a few of the top reasons why electronic books are replacing paperbacks for many avid readers.

As always, Ellora's Cave and Cerridwen Press welcome your questions and comments. We invite you to email us at Comments@ellorascave.com or write to us directly at Ellora's Cave Publishing Inc., 1056 Home Avenue, Akron, OH 44310-3502.

COMING TO A BOOKSTORE NEAR YOU!

ELLORA'S CAVE

Bestselling Authors Tour

UPDATES AVAILABLE AT

WWW.ELLORASCAVE.COM

erridwen, the Celtic Goddess of wisdom, was the muse who brought inspiration to storytellers and those in the creative arts. Cerridwen Press encompasses the best and most innovative stories in all genres of today's fiction. Visit our site and discover the newest titles by talented authors who still get inspired - much like the ancient storytellers did, once upon a time.

Cerridwen Press

www.cerridwenpress.com